HARLEQUIN®
Presents

The last, hazy days of August are meant for basking in the sun and reading good books. Whether you're relaxing in your backyard, on your porch or maybe chilling on vacation, make sure to have a selection of Harlequin Presents titles by your side. We've got eight great novels to choose from....

Bestselling author Lynne Graham presents her latest tale of a mistress who's forced to marry an Italian billionaire in *Mistress Bought and Paid For*. And Miranda Lee is as steamy as ever with her long-awaited romp, *Love-Slave to the Sheikh*, for our hot UNCUT miniseries.

You never know what goes on behind closed doors, and we have three very different stories about marriages to prove it: Anne Mather's sexy and emotional *Jack Riordan's Baby* will have your heart in your mouth while also tugging at its strings, while *Bought by Her Husband*, Sharon Kendrick's newest release, and Kate Walker's *The Antonakos Marriage* are two slices of Greek tycoon heaven with spicy twists!

If it's something more traditional you're after, we've plenty of choice: *By Royal Demand*, the first installment in Robyn Donald's new regal saga, THE ROYAL HOUSE OF ILLYRIA, won't disappoint. Or you might like to try *The Italian Millionaire's Virgin Wife* by Diana Hamilton and *His Very Personal Assistant* by Carole Mortimer— two shy, sensible, prim-and-proper women find themselves living lives they've never dreamed of when they attract two rich, arrogant and darkly handsome men!

Enjoy!

In Love with Her Boss

*Getting to know him in the boardroom—
and the bedroom!*

**A secret romance, a forbidden affair,
a thrilling attraction...**

**What happens when two people work together
and simply can't help falling in love—
no matter how hard they try to resist?**

**Find out in our popular series of stories
set in the world of work.**

**This month, Carole Mortimer tugs heartstrings
with her intense, emotional story of a personal
assistant who has fallen secretly in love with
her handsome, reputedly womanizing boss!**

Available only from Harlequin Presents®

Coming in October:

The Playboy Boss's Chosen Bride
by Emma Darcy
#2572

Carole Mortimer

HIS VERY PERSONAL ASSISTANT

In Love
With Her
Boss

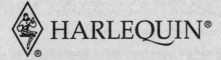

HARLEQUIN®

TORONTO • NEW YORK • LONDON
AMSTERDAM • PARIS • SYDNEY • HAMBURG
STOCKHOLM • ATHENS • TOKYO • MILAN • MADRID
PRAGUE • WARSAW • BUDAPEST • AUCKLAND

ISBN-13: 978-0-373-12562-3
ISBN-10:   0-373-12562-3

HIS VERY PERSONAL ASSISTANT

First North American Publication 2006.

www.eHarlequin.com

Printed in U.S.A.

All about the author...
Carole Mortimer

CAROLE MORTIMER is one of Harlequin's most popular and prolific authors. Since her first novel published in 1979, this British writer has shown no signs of slowing her pace. In fact, she has published more than 125 books to date!

Carole was born in a village in England; she claims it was so small that "if you blinked as you drove through it you could miss seeing it completely!" She adds that her parents still live in the house where she was born, and her two brothers live very close by.

Carole's early ambition to become a nurse came to an abrupt end after only one year of training due to a weakness in her back, suffered after a fall. Instead she went on to work in the computer department of a well-known stationery company.

During her time there, Carole made her first attempt at writing a novel for Harlequin. "The manuscript was far too short and the plotline not up to standard, so I naturally received a rejection slip," she says. "Not taking rejection well, I went off in a sulk for two years before deciding to have another go." Her second manuscript was accepted, beginning a long and fruitful career. She says she has "enjoyed every moment of it!"

Carole lives "in a most beautiful part of Britain" with her husband and children.

"I really do enjoy my writing, and have every intention of continuing to do so for another twenty years!"

For Peter

CHAPTER ONE

'I WOULD like to strangle that woman with one of her diamond necklaces!'

Kit looked up as her outer office door opened, inwardly wincing as it was thrown back with such force that it slammed against the wall. Inwardly, because outwardly she always remained the calm and efficient personal assistant that she was...

She raised enquiring brows as her boss, Marcus Maitland, strode purposefully across the room to his own office, receiving a narrow-eyed glare for her efforts, his handsome face harsh and grimly set.

'I don't want to be disturbed,' he bit out gratingly as he wrenched open his own office door. 'By anyone,' he added forcefully, slamming that door behind him with equal force.

Kit breathed out slowly, turning to Lewis Grant, the lawyer for Maitland Enterprises, as he entered the room. 'I take it the meeting with Angus Gerrard didn't go as planned?' she prompted softly.

'Not exactly.' Lewis grimaced as he sat on the edge of her desk to look across at the blankness of the door so recently closed in both their faces. He was tall and blond and in his early thirties.

Marcus and Lewis had set out earlier for their meeting with Angus Gerrard believing the takeover of the other man's newspaper empire was only a formality; a mere signing of the papers was to be performed. But, from Marcus's comment when he'd come in, and his obvious fury, Kit had a feeling that it had been far from a formality!

'Nothing that you did or didn't do, I hope?' Because she also knew, from six months of working as Marcus Maitland's personal assistant, that he worked so hard himself he was not a man to accept incompetence or compromise in others.

Not that she could blame him; as a multimillionaire, involved in numerous diversified companies and holdings, he had little time to spare for other people's mistakes.

'No—thank goodness!' Lewis gave a rueful grin.

'The lady he wants to strangle with her diamond necklace?' Kit prompted knowingly.

Lewis nodded. 'Catherine Grainger.'

Exactly whom Kit had thought Marcus was referring to. But had hoped that he wasn't.

She hadn't known of it when she'd started working for Marcus Maitland, but there seemed to be some sort of long-running competitiveness between Maitland Enterprises and Grainger International. Catherine Grainger was the major shareholder and head of the latter. In the six months that Kit had worked for Marcus Maitland this was the third time the two of them seemed to have locked horns over a business acquisition.

Kit grimaced. 'What happened this time?'

Lewis shrugged. 'She outbid and outmanoeuvred us. Angus Gerrard signed a contract with her yesterday,' he enlarged as Kit continued to look at him.

'Oops!' she breathed slowly.

'Oops, indeed,' Lewis acknowledged as he continued to stare at the door Marcus had closed so decisively behind him minutes ago. 'You know, Marcus mentioned this is the third time this has happened in the last few months,' he said slowly.

Kit looked up at him enquiringly as his words echoed her own recent thoughts.

'It's probably nothing,' Lewis dismissed briskly as he stood up. 'There's obviously no point in my hanging around here—' he smiled wryly '—so I may as well get back to my own office—if only to shred these defunct contracts!' He picked up his briefcase from beside Kit's desk before leaving for his own office further down the carpeted corridor.

Kit was still frowning as she watched him go. Surely it was all a coincidence that Marcus Maitland had lost yet another deal because Catherine Grainger had outmanoeuvred him…? To attribute the blame to anything else was surely to bring into question the integrity of everyone who worked closely with Marcus Maitland. Including herself.

'Daydreaming, Miss McGuire?' a female voice queried nastily. 'Does that mean that Marcus isn't back yet?' Andrea Revel added as she strolled into Kit's office completely unannounced, bringing the aroma of her heavy perfume with her.

Kit kept her expression deliberately bland, knowing that it wouldn't be her secretary, Laura's, fault that this woman had managed to get in here without interference. The latest in what appeared to have been a long line of women in Marcus Maitland's life, Andrea Revel seemed to think she was a law unto herself when it came to Marcus.

The other woman was astoundingly beautiful, with

her pale blonde hair, slanted green eyes and a figure that had all the men in her immediate vicinity turning to admire her, especially as she usually wore some stunning creation or another. As a fashion buyer for one of the most prestigious stores in the city, Andrea had no problem finding or buying such clothing.

But Andrea also had to be one of the most unpleasant women Kit had ever met, and hard as nails with it. At least, away from Marcus Maitland she was. When in his presence, Andrea somehow contrived to look small, vulnerable, and completely feminine.

However, Kit refused to rise to the bait about sitting around daydreaming while her boss was out of the office. 'Actually, he's back—'

'Oh, good.' Andrea smiled as she turned towards Marcus's office, showing even white teeth behind the glossy red lipstick she wore, which matched her short, fitted dress.

'But he doesn't want to be disturbed,' Kit added firmly as she stood up.

Andrea gave her a dismissive glance. 'He'll want to see me,' she said confidently, reaching for the door handle. 'Go away,' she bit out impatiently as Kit tried to move smoothly in front of her. 'You take your duties as Marcus's PA too seriously, as far as I'm concerned,' she added scathingly. 'In fact, I've told Marcus as much on several occasions.'

Kit drew herself up to her full height of five feet ten inches and looked at Andrea down the length of her nose as she breathed deeply in an effort to stop a cutting reply from leaving her lips. Andrea might be gone from Marcus's life in a matter of months—in fact, to Kit's disapproval, the secretaries in the company were taking bets as to how long this particular relationship was going to last!—but in the meantime she had to attempt to be polite to her. Even if sometimes she did inwardly feel like wiping that superior smile off the other woman's face!

'It doesn't seem to have affected my current employment,' Kit finally returned in a pleasant voice—not quite succeeding in hiding her resentment, after all.

Green eyes narrowed venomously. 'Why, you—'

'I'll just ask Mr Maitland if he is free to see you now,' Kit continued lightly, opening the door to Marcus's office and closing it firmly behind her. After all, this was nothing personal, just part of her job.

But that certainly hadn't been her most successful attempt at handling Andrea Revel, she inwardly berated herself as Marcus raised his head to look scowlingly across at her for her intrusion.

At the age of thirty-nine, Marcus Maitland had to be one of the most handsome men Kit had ever seen, with that midnight-dark hair and deep blue eyes. His nose was a straight slash, his lips sculptured, his chin square and determined. But she made sure always to regard him with cool impassivity.

Because she had been warned by Angie Dwyer, this man's previous PA, when she had come for her interview for the job seven months ago, that the worst possible thing she could do was to fall for Marcus—that he *never* fell in love with any of the women he was involved with, his relationships with them only ever lasting a couple of months.

Considering the circumstances that had forced Kit to leave her last job—her boss seemed to have considered it normal policy to be involved with his assistant—

she'd had no intention of falling in love with Marcus. Until she had actually met the man himself. Then she'd had trouble believing that any woman within a twenty-mile radius could actually stop herself from being attracted to him!

The term 'tall, dark and handsome' definitely applied to Marcus Maitland, but there was so much else that was attractive about him too. For one thing—when he wasn't furiously angry, as he was this morning, he was capable of charming even the hardest heart, and his wealth and success had given him a self-confidence that made him stand out in any crowd.

In a word, Marcus Maitland was *gorgeous*!

But Kit took great care never to let him see what she really thought of him.

Besides, having taken account of Angie Dwyer's warning, Kit played down her own looks when at work, wearing her copper-coloured hair in a French pleat, keeping her make-up minimal, discarding her contact lenses for thick-rimmed glasses during the day in an effort to lessen the effect of the deep grey of her eyes and surrounding dark lashes. The jackets of the dark business suits she wore were shapeless, the skirts always discreetly knee-length and her shoes low-heeled.

There was no way, she had decided, after looking at her reflection in the mirror that first morning she had come to work here, that any man seeing her like this would consider it part of her job to keep his bed warm if they should happen to be away on business together!

Kit had spent too long running round desks, and hotel bedrooms, trying to avoid her previous boss's less-than-welcome advances, to want a repeat of it in her new job.

Although once she had actually met Marcus Maitland she hadn't been quite so sure about that…!

Still, she had deliberately chosen her role as demure, plain, featureless, figureless Kit McGuire, and so far she had stuck to it.

But a few more conversations like the one just now with Andrea Revel, and she might just decide to throw caution to the wind and—

No, she wouldn't, she gently rebuked herself; she enjoyed her work here, the people she worked with, the man she worked for, and most important of all— she needed the job! Besides, how would it look on her c.v. if, when she applied for another position, she had to own up to being dismissed for insubordination to her boss's girlfriend?

But it would be nice, just for once, if Marcus could see what she looked like when away from the office, with her hair loose, no glasses to hide the luminous depths of her eyes, a pair of denims that fitted snugly to—

'Well?' Marcus snapped harshly, tapping his fingers impatiently on his desk top as he continued to wait for an explanation for her intrusion after he had explicitly told her he didn't want to be disturbed.

At the same time completely bursting Kit's bubble of illusion where, as in Hollywood movies, Marcus saw her change from a moth into a butterfly and instantly fell in love with the way she really looked. A fairy tale!

She straightened. 'Miss Revel would like to see you,' she told him briskly.

'When?'

'Now. She's waiting outside in my office,' she explained as he continued to scowl.

His brow cleared. 'Then why didn't you tell me that when you first came in?' He stood up to move impatiently around her and open the inter-office door himself. 'Come in, Andrea,' he invited. 'I was going to call you in a few minutes anyway; I have something I need to discuss with you.'

Kit stiffened as the other woman gave her a triumphant look in passing, her hands closing at her sides, her jaw clenching. Andrea deliberately went to link her arm with Marcus's, before standing on tiptoe to kiss him lingeringly on the mouth.

Kit felt her stomach turn as Marcus bent his head with the intention of returning the kiss, quickly turning on her heel and leaving the room, closing the door behind her to lean weakly back against it.

So much for Angie Dwyer's warning!

Kit had known by the end of the first week of working with Marcus that she was deeply attracted to him. Not the cleverest thing she had ever done in her life, but probably not the worst either. After all, Marcus had no idea how she felt, so at least her pride was still intact. It was only her heart that went AWOL every time she looked at him!

Only...!

She gave a self-deriding shake of her head as she moved back to sit behind her desk. It was probably as well that she could laugh at her own stupidity, because over the last six months Andrea Revel was the third woman Kit had seen Marcus get involved with—and they had all, without exception, been aged in their mid-thirties, petite, blonde, and curvaceously feminine—not twenty-six, tall and slim, with red hair.

In other words, even without the severe hairstyle, no make-up, and the shapeless business suits she wore, she just wasn't Marcus Maitland's type. It was—

'Give me a call when you get back,' Andrea Revel snapped as she suddenly stormed out of the inner office. 'I may decide to see you again—but then, I may have something else more important to do!' she ended before slamming the door behind her. Her face was an ugly, angry mask as she leant over Kit's desk to thrust it inches away from Kit's. 'You think you're so clever, don't you?' she hissed furiously as Kit could only blink her surprise at the attack. 'But we'll see who has the last laugh,' she scorned as she straightened and, with one last flounce of her rich blonde hair, swayed provocatively from the room.

Now what on earth had all that been about? Kit wondered dazedly as she watched her leave, slightly shaken by the vehemence behind the woman.

The door to Marcus's office opened again, gently this time. He stood framed in the doorway. 'Has she gone?' he enquired.

'Are you referring to Miss Revel?' Kit prompted innocently.

His gaze narrowed as he looked at her assessingly, a smile tugging at the corners of that sensuously curved mouth. 'Yes, I'm referring to Miss Revel,' he confirmed dryly, his earlier fury seeming to have abated as his normal good humour asserted itself.

Kit gave a slight inclination of her head. 'She appears to have gone, yes,' she confirmed evenly, still feeling totally stunned by Andrea's verbal attack.

Marcus's eyes gleamed deeply blue as he looked at her consideringly. 'You know, Miss McGuire, sometimes I'm not sure you're altogether quite what you seem…'

She remained outwardly composed, but inwardly her stomach was clenched, her thoughts were racing. What if he knew…what if he had guessed at her connection to…? But there was absolutely no reason why he should have done, she instantly consoled herself.

'Miss Revel seemed—upset, when she left just now?' she said briskly, deliberately changing the subject.

Marcus smiled more openly now, leaning against the doorframe to fold his arms across his chest. 'Furious, you mean?' he drawled.

'Well…yes,' Kit confirmed coolly.

He gave an acknowledging inclination of his head, his hair gleaming blue-black in the overhead light. 'Your fault, I'm afraid,' he derided.

Her eyes widened. 'Mine? But—I was only doing my job just now,' she defended. 'Besides, she was rude to me first,' she added quietly.

Marcus raised dark brows. 'She was?'

'Yes, she—' She broke off, her frown deepening as she realised from his curious expression that he had no idea what she was talking about. 'Exactly why is Miss Revel furious with me?' she asked slowly.

He shrugged broad shoulders beneath the white silk shirt and dark tailored jacket he wore. 'She's taken exception—and I very much doubt we will see each other again—to the fact that you're the one coming away with me this weekend rather than her.'

Kit stared at him blankly.

When had he—
When had they—
When had she—
What on earth was he talking about?

CHAPTER TWO

'WELL, Marcus's last PA did warn you that you might have to go away on business with him occasionally,' Penny, Kit's flatmate, teased her later that evening as the two of them prepared a meal together.

Yes, Angie Dwyer had told Kit that travelling with Marcus Maitland on business was part of her job description; it was just that it hadn't been an issue over the last six months because, until this weekend, Marcus had preferred to take Lewis with him when he went on a trip.

Not that going away on business with Marcus Maitland was actually a problem. It was just the way he had told her and then chuckled at her stunned reaction that had thrown her slightly.

In fact, a lot!

'Don't look so worried, Miss McGuire,' Marcus had grinned as she'd stared across the office at him after his announcement that he and Andrea Revel had parted company, and that he was taking Kit away for the weekend with him. 'I'm not suggesting that I'm about to make indecent advances upon your person,' he'd told her mockingly. 'I just happen to need your capabilities more this weekend than I do Andrea's rather more obvious charms!'

Kit hadn't been too sure she found that an altogether flattering summing-up of the situation, but as she had made a point of deliberately playing down her own looks there wasn't too much she could say in her own defence.

What would Marcus say if he could see her now? she wondered. Her hair was loose like silken flame past her shoulders, her skimpy tee shirt and fitted denims clung to her slender curves and there were no heavy glasses, either, to hide the large deep grey eyes that were surrounded by thick dark lashes. She looked a good ten years younger than the primly efficient Miss McGuire!

But knowing Marcus's preference for tiny blondes, he probably still wouldn't be impressed, she allowed ruefully.

'So where exactly are the two of you going this weekend?' Penny enquired with deliberate innocence as she sliced up tomatoes to go in a salad.

Kit paused in opening a bottle of wine to wince at her friend's teasing. 'We aren't going anywhere,' she corrected irritably. 'Marcus has accepted an invitation from Desmond Hayes—'

'The airline tycoon, Desmond Hayes?' Penny cut in speculatively, blue eyes glowing interestedly.

'Is there another one?' Kit came back evenly— briefly enjoying her moment of glory as she could see that her friend and flatmate was impressed by the name of their host for the weekend.

'None that matter,' Penny acknowledged. 'Wow. So you're going to be spending the weekend with Desmond Hayes,' she admired enviously.

Kit pursed her lips. 'I am no more spending the weekend with Desmond Hayes than I am with Marcus Maitland; this is simply a working trip,' she stated firmly.

'Yes, but you're still going to be there, alone, with two of the most gorgeous men—'

'There's apparently going to be a few other people staying too over the weekend,' Kit quickly interrupted.

'Stop bursting my bubble!' Penny exclaimed disgruntledly, taking a sip from her glass of wine before looking sharply at Kit. 'Don't, for goodness' sake, tell me that you're going there as Miss McGuire, the PA from No-Nonsenseville? You are, aren't you?' she accused incredulously as she saw Kit's raised brows. 'Oh, Kit, you can't—'

'Of course I can,' Kit said a little crossly. 'This is a *working* trip, Penny, in case you've forgotten—'

'I haven't forgotten anything,' her friend assured her seriously. 'And, after the shenanigans with Mike Reynolds while you worked for him, I can't exactly blame you for being more cautious where Marcus Maitland is concerned. But you've been his assistant for six months, Kit; surely you know what sort of man he is by now?'

Oh, yes, she knew exactly what sort of man Marcus Maitland was: clever and shrewd where business was concerned, a fair but demanding boss. But, as Angie Dwyer had warned her, he changed his women almost as often as he changed his shirt.

'You're going to meet Desmond Hayes this weekend,' Penny said impatiently. 'Desmond Hayes, Kit; one of the wealthiest men in the country!'

Kit gave a faint smile. 'He may be, but the last I heard he was on his third marriage!'

'No, that's been over for some months,' Penny dismissed.

Kit gave a firm shake of her head. 'Then he's in the

middle of a messy divorce,' she persisted. 'In either case, I'm not interested. Neither,' she continued firmly as Penny would have spoken, 'do I intend changing a single thing about my appearance for what is, after all, a work commitment.' If she kept repeating that phrase enough, she might even start to believe it herself!

Because a part of her was secretly excited at the thought of spending this time with Marcus away from the office—safely behind the façade of the PA from No-Nonsenseville, of course!

Penny gave an exasperated sigh. 'Well, for what it's worth, I think you're insane!'

Kit gave a smile. 'I'll try to bear that in mind.'

'Insane!' Penny repeated disgustedly before picking up the salad bowl and sweeping over to the kitchen table, leaving Kit to follow slowly behind her with the plates of baked salmon.

Maybe, feeling as she did about Marcus, she was mad to keep up this charade of efficient primness, but having started it she now had no idea how to finish it...

'I beg your pardon?' Kit looked at Marcus incredulously when he called for her the next afternoon, having allowed her to leave the office earlier so that she might be ready for the two of them to make the journey to Desmond Hayes's home.

He gave a sigh. 'I said, could you change into something a little less—formal?' he repeated tersely, eyeing her cream linen suit and flat shoes with obvious distaste. 'Desmond is expecting my partner for the weekend to be the current woman in my life, not my PA,' he explained with the deliberate patience of an adult talking to a recalcitrant child.

'But—but—'

'Now you sound like a broken record,' Marcus drawled derisively, moving past her into the flat's hall-way.

Penny was, thankfully, still at work; otherwise there was no knowing what she might have made of what Marcus was asking.

Kit wasn't too sure of that herself! Exactly what did he mean, she was supposed to be the current woman in his life and not his PA? Surely he wasn't suggest-ing—?

'Calm down, Miss McGuire,' Marcus ordered as he stood in the hallway looking down at her—a novelty in itself: at five feet ten inches tall, Kit usually found she was taller than most men. 'I only said Desmond Hayes is expecting you to be the woman I'm involved with—not that I am expecting it too!'

She could feel the warmth of colour enter her cheeks at his taunting tone and mocking expression. But how else could she react after what he had just said?

Marcus gave another sigh. 'It's quite simple, Miss McGuire, I look on this weekend as purely business. Desmond may see it a little differently, hence—'

'Hence you want me to appear to be your girlfriend,' Kit finished dazedly.

'There you are.' Marcus smiled teasingly. 'I knew you would get it in the end!'

She hadn't got anything!

This was the very first time Marcus had mentioned anything about this particular aspect of the weekend.

Deliberately so? she wondered as she looked at him suspiciously.

His smile turned to a scowl. 'As I told you yesterday, I'm not about to make indecent advances on your person!' he told her disgustedly.

But Kit hadn't needed him to repeat it, knew that he didn't find her in the least attractive; she just couldn't make too much sense of what he was saying. It appeared that Marcus had originally intended going with Andrea to Desmond Hayes's for the weekend—the woman's vehemence yesterday at being told she wasn't going after all was proof of that!—so why was he now taking Kit, but still leaving his host with the impression it was his girlfriend who was accompanying him?

'It's simple enough, Miss McGuire—'

'You keep saying that,' she cut in tensely.

'But you don't find it so,' Marcus replied through gritted teeth. 'I swear, I want your experience as my PA this weekend, not as a woman.'

'That part you've made abundantly clear!' she snapped back, slightly disconcerted as Marcus gave her an assessing look for her vehemence. 'And quite rightly so,' she added hastily. 'But what is it you want me—as your PA—to do?' she persisted, desperately trying to claw back some of the credibility she was sure she had lost just now when she had sounded almost disappointed that Marcus wanted her services professionally but not personally.

Idiot, she chided herself. As if Marcus could ever have any personal interest in her.

'Observe and listen, mainly,' he answered in a casual voice. 'There are rumours that Desmond Hayes is in trouble—financially, for a change, as opposed to the mess he's made of his personal life. Three wives!' he added with a disgusted shake of his head.

'I suppose you think he shouldn't have married those women at all but just—er—what I meant—' Kit broke off abruptly, wincing awkwardly as she realised what she had been about to say, the colour once again hot in her cheeks.

'But just bedded them—like me,' Marcus finished for her. 'Was that what you were about to say?'

It was. Though it had dawned on her just how unwise she was being before she had even finished saying it. Although that didn't stop Marcus from being completely aware of what she had been about to say, anyway!

'You know, Miss McGuire,' he murmured, the humour once more lighting the deep blue of his eyes, 'perhaps this weekend will serve another purpose, after all. You've been working for me for six months now, and it's time I got to know you a little better,' he enlightened her as she looked at him warily.

Having Marcus get to know her a little or, indeed, a lot better, was not something she particularly wanted!

She deliberately avoided his gaze now. 'What do the rumours have to say about Desmond Hayes's financial problems?' she prompted, determined to take the conversation onto a more businesslike footing.

'So far, only that he's in trouble. I want to see if we can't find out a little more about that over this weekend.'

'And you don't think Miss Revel would have been able to help you with that better than I?' Kit replied, sure that the kittenish Andrea would be much more successful at persuading Desmond Hayes, a man with an obvious weakness for beautiful women, into talking about himself and his problems.

Poor Penny, too; she would be most disappointed to hear that Desmond Hayes might no longer be one of the richest men in England!

Marcus's mouth thinned. 'My relationship with Andrea is over,' he bit out decisively. 'Besides, I've always made it a rule to keep my personal and my private life completely separate.'

'Strange, I'd heard differently—' Kit gave an uncomfortable wince as she realised what she had just said.

'From whom, may I ask?' he demanded.

'Someone mentioned it. I forget who,' Kit said firmly as he gave her a disbelieving look.

His smile was humourless. 'Angie always did have a big mouth,' he ruminated. 'It's one of the reasons she didn't work out too well as my previous PA. Whereas you...'

Kit arched dark brows. 'Me?'

Marcus gave her an appreciative smile. 'You're so discreet that even your own personal life is a closed book! This is a nice apartment, by the way.' He looked around them admiringly. 'Very minimalistic,' he approved. The bare wooden floors were adorned with brightly coloured scatter rugs rather than a carpet, and there was just a cream sofa, chair and bookcase in the sitting-room, which he could see from the hallway. 'Very nice,' he repeated slowly. 'Perhaps I'm paying you too much.' He eyed her with challenging amusement.

Kit had been reeling from his comment about her personal life being a closed book, but this comment about her apartment, coming so close on its heels, made her frown darkly. 'I happen to share this apartment,' she told him sharply. 'And you certainly do not pay me too much!'

Marcus laughed, his teeth very white and even against his tanned skin, his eyes gleaming deeply blue. 'I thought even you might have something to say about that,' he responded.

'Even me?' she rejoined, wondering exactly what he had meant by that remark.

'Well, as I've already said, you've worked for me for six months or so now, and I still know very little about you.'

And he wasn't going to know anything about her either, if she had her way! Most of it was pretty boring, and what wasn't boring was pretty damning—as far as Marcus was concerned, she intended her life should remain a closed book!

'I see nothing wrong in that,' she told him tartly. 'The only things I know about your personal life would be better left unknown—' She broke off abruptly, realising she had yet again overstepped the line she had drawn between them when she had first started working for him. 'Sorry,' she muttered, looking away.

Marcus eyed her assessingly. 'No, you're not,' he said comfortably. 'You said you share this apartment?' he continued.

One of the things she most admired about this man was his intelligence—though she wasn't quite so sure about that when it was directed towards her! She had thought he hadn't paid any particular notice to her comment about sharing the apartment, but he had simply been saving his curiosity for the right moment. Like now.

'Yes,' she answered unhelpfully. 'Now, what is it you want me to wear this weekend, if not my business clothes?' She noted his own casual black denims and dark blue shirt open at the throat.

'Anything but,' he responded. 'What you have on is okay—if you were going to pay a visit on an aged relative! And I'm sure those suits you wear to the office are very smart—'

'But?' Kit interjected guardedly, already stung by his comment about the cream linen suit she was wearing. Though the four dark suits that she usually wore to work were sensible, they were smart of their kind—and had been expensive too.

'But they aren't suitable for a summer weekend in the country,' Marcus persisted unapologetically. 'For instance, have you packed a bikini?'

'Certainly not!'

'Well, Desmond has a full-sized outdoor heated swimming pool. Plus a stable if you happen to ride—'

'I don't.' Kit did her best to repress a shudder just at the thought of getting on a horse; they were truly magnificent creatures to look at—from a distance!—but too unpredictable for her taste. 'I like to go for walks, though,' she said lightly, starting to wonder if this weekend might not be fun, after all.

'Then you'll need a pair of walking boots, and so do I,' Marcus informed her happily. 'And a pair of jeans and some tops to relax in during the day, plus something a bit more glamorous for dinner in the evenings—'

'Okay, okay.' Kit held up her hands in self-defence. 'I get the picture.'

'Good.' Marcus nodded his satisfaction. 'Off you go and change, and repack your suitcase, then. I'll just sit in here and look through your book collection while I'm waiting,' he informed her arrogantly, before strolling into the sitting-room to do exactly that.

Kit stared after him frustratedly. She might, as she said, get the picture, but how on earth was she supposed to keep up the prim Miss McGuire role wearing denims—or worse!—a bikini?

CHAPTER THREE

'THAT'S better!' Marcus voiced his approval when Kit rejoined him in the sitting-room fifteen minutes later.

Fifteen *agonizing* minutes later. Kit simply hadn't known what to do for the best once she was in her bedroom. If she did as Marcus asked, and dressed and behaved as casually as he was himself, wasn't that going to make a nonsense of the working relationship she had gone to such lengths to establish the last six months? But on the other hand, if she didn't fulfil her role as his PA, Marcus wasn't going to think she was of much use to him, and maybe he'd decide, as he obviously had with Angie Dwyer, that she wasn't working out too well.

Besides, as he had gone to great pains to point out, he had no designs upon her body!

Not sure whether she felt relieved, chagrined, or just plain disappointed about that, Kit had taken a quick inventory of her wardrobe and had picked out the clothing she thought might do for the occasion, without compromising herself too much. From the look on Marcus's face as he looked at her now in a black tee shirt and fashionable fitted black trousers, he obviously approved of the transformation.

'At least,' he said as he slowly stood up, 'the clothes are. Can't you do something with your hair?' He glowered at the severe style she still wore. 'And the glasses?'

he added with exasperation. 'Desmond is going to think my taste has turned to the studious!'

'As opposed to dumb blondes!' Kit was stung into retorting, the colour swiftly entering her cheeks as Marcus turned to look at her beneath lowered lids. 'I'm so sorry!' she gasped. 'I really shouldn't have said that. I just— You were being extremely personal about me, and so—'

'You felt the freedom to be extremely personal about me, in return,' Marcus drawled.

She grimaced. 'Yes.'

'Fair enough,' he agreed.

Her eyes widened in surprise. She had expected a verbal setting-down, if nothing else. 'It is?'

'Of course,' he said. 'Although I wouldn't advise you to do it too often!'

Kit stared at him for several seconds, and then she gave a laugh as she saw the glint in his dark blue eyes.

Marcus tilted his head as he looked at her consideringly. 'Is that really how you see the women I've been involved with?' he asked quizzically.

In truth, yes. Oh, they were beautiful enough, but Kit very much doubted that their conversation had run to much more than fashion and social chit chat. Not exactly scintillating to a man of Marcus's intelligence. Although she very much doubted it was intellect that had attracted him to them!

'Perhaps,' she answered noncommittally. 'Although I really don't know them well enough to comment, do I?'

'That doesn't seem to have stopped you doing exactly that, anyway,' Marcus pointed out dryly.

No, it hadn't, had it? Kit realised, the colour once

more in her cheeks. And it really wasn't any of her business, was it...?

She put up a self-conscious hand to her hair, aware that its vibrancy of colour was mostly muted by its severe style; that it glowed like flame when released, sometimes deeply red, sometimes that red hinting at gold, at other times just pure gold. As for discarding her glasses...!

'Which brings us back to your hair,' Marcus said firmly as he saw her nervous movement. 'It looks like okay hair to me.'

'It is,' she confirmed awkwardly.

'Then why not let it down for a change? Just your hair, Miss McGuire,' he added as he recognized his choice of words could be misinterpreted. 'And do you really need those glasses?' He reached out as if to pluck them off her nose. 'The lenses don't look very strong to me—hey, I was only going to look at them!' he protested as she swung away from his hand.

'You might break them,' she said stiltedly, reaching up herself to remove the glasses; she had her contacts with her, could put them in later. 'I really only need them for reading,' she excused, her face turned away as she put the glasses carefully into their case and into her handbag.

'Miss McGuire...?'

'Yes?' she replied distractedly.

'Would you mind looking at me when I talk to you?'

'What—?' She broke off as she turned and saw the look on Marcus's face. He was staring at her, which sent the colour once more to flush her cheeks.

And she knew what he would see too; eyes of deep gun-metal grey, but with the softness of velvet, her lashes long and dark, those eyes emphasizing her high cheekbones, the perfect bow of her lips.

Marcus blinked. 'Could you take down your hair, too?' he pressed huskily.

She gave an irritated groan. 'Look, I really don't think this is at all necessary—'

'Please,' he pushed gently.

Kit shot him an uncertain glance before looking away again, reaching up to remove the pins from her hair, its straight, silky softness falling gently about her shoulders, the sunlight streaming in through the window giving it the texture of living flame.

'There.' She raised her chin as she looked at him, flicking her hair back over her shoulder as she did so. 'Satisfied?'

Marcus put a hand up to absently stroke the roughness of his chin as he continued to look at her with enigmatic eyes. 'As a matter of fact—no, I'm far from satisfied!' he replied. 'What I am, though, is curious as to why you've been walking around my office the last six months masquerading as someone's maiden aunt, when, in actual fact, you really look like this!'

Kit continued to look at him with steady grey eyes. 'Like what?'

He looked ready to explode. 'Like—like—'

'Yes?' she prompted curiously.

'You know exactly what you look like, Miss McGuire,' he bit out coldly. 'What I want to know is why?'

She avoided meeting his gaze. 'If you really must know—'

'Oh, I think I really must,' he assured sarcastically.

Kit took a deep breath. 'My previous boss thought

it part of my job description to go to bed with him. And after Angie Dwyer's comments about you, I—well, I thought it best not to draw attention to—to my femininity,' she concluded awkwardly.

'In other words, you didn't draw my attention to it!' Marcus rasped furiously. 'Damn it, have I so much as looked at you in a way that could be called personal in the last six months?'

'No,' she acknowledged with a pained grimace, knowing his anger was justified.

'You—I—oh, to hell with this,' he suddenly said impatiently. 'If you're ready, let's just go, shall we?' He turned on his heel and walked out of her apartment.

Kit breathed a sigh of relief at being released from his domineering company for a couple of minutes at least, the tension relaxing from her shoulders. Marcus obviously wasn't a happy man at what he saw to be her transition from moth into butterfly, or the reason for it. As she had known he wouldn't be...

Oh, well. She gave a philosophical shrug of her shoulders as she picked up her bag and followed him out to his car; he had asked for it, hadn't he? He could hardly sack her just because she had turned out to be more attractive without her hair confined and not wearing her glasses than he had actually bargained for!

'Where, exactly, are we going?' she asked after ten minutes of silent driving on Marcus's part—and, she admitted, a certain amount of discomfort on hers!

'Worcestershire,' he supplied economically.

'Really?' She brightened. 'I've never been there, but I believe it's supposed to be a very pretty county—'

'Would you mind not chattering?' Marcus cut in hardly. 'I need to concentrate while I'm driving.'

He needed to learn some manners too—but somehow Kit didn't think he would appreciate having her point that out to him!

But if he didn't want to talk, she was quite happy to look out the window at the countryside as they left London far behind them, the Jaguar sports car Marcus drove quickly eating up the miles.

She'd had all too few opportunities to get out of London since selling her car six months ago, driving and parking in the city simply weren't worth the nightmare. Her parents lived in Cornwall, and it was easier to get on the train when she went to see them than it was to struggle through all the tourist traffic that constantly clogged the roads down there.

'Okay, I apologize for my brusqueness,' Marcus said suddenly beside her, startling her out of her reverie.

Kit tilted her chin up as she looked at him. 'Which time?'

His hands tightened on the steering wheel as he glanced back at her.

'Both times,' he acknowledged. 'I admit, I was initially a little—startled, by the change in your appearance—even more so by the reason for the subterfuge in the first place.' He looked darkly at the road ahead. 'Talk if you want to,' he commanded.

Kit continued to watch him for several long seconds, finding that, now he had invited her to talk, she actually had nothing to say!

'Well?' he persisted tersely at her continued silence.

She gave a rueful laugh. 'Isn't it strange, that when someone invites you to talk, there's really nothing to talk about? But if I think of anything, I'll certainly say it,' she amended hastily at the frown line remaining between his eyes.

Marcus gave a small smile. 'I'm gratified to hear it!'

'No, you aren't,' she said with certainty. 'And I'm really quite happy just looking out of the window,' she assured him. 'It's easy to forget, living in London, just how beautiful England really is.'

'Yes,' he answered shortly. 'Tell me a little about yourself, Miss McGuire,' he invited. 'I ought to know something about the woman I'm spending the weekend with, don't you think?'

'I suppose,' she acknowledged reluctantly, not sure how much she wanted this man to know about her. Always a private person, she now found it more important than ever to keep personal information to a minimum—considering this man's connections...

'You suppose?' he echoed slightly incredulously. 'Miss McGuire, I'm not asking for intimate details; just a general outline will do! Things like parents and siblings; after all, your résumé has already told me about your previous employment, educational qualifications and marital status!'

'Oh, good,' she said sarcastically. 'Well, I have two parents: a mother and a father—'

'I'm glad to hear it!' he drawled with derisive patience, 'why is it I get the feeling you really don't want to talk about your private life?'

'Probably because I don't,' she answered candidly. 'But I'm quite happy for you to tell me about yours, if you feel so inclined?' She looked at him expectantly.

He flicked her another glance with those deep blue eyes. 'You know, I think you might be a lot less trouble as the supremely efficient Miss McGuire; she tends not to answer back!'

Kit grinned self-consciously. 'Sorry.'

'No, you're not. And, for the record, I have a mother and a father, too,' he continued wryly.

'Well, at least we have that much in common, Mr Maitland—'

'Marcus,' he insisted. 'I think that might sound a little less—formal, for the benefit of this weekend, don't you?' He raised mocking brows.

She hesitated for a moment. 'You know, I really don't think you thought the consequences of this weekend through enough before deciding on your plan of action—'

'You don't?' His brows rose higher.

'No, I don't.' Kit turned fully in her seat to look at him. 'For one thing,' she continued determinedly as he would have interrupted, 'how are we supposed to go back to being Mr Maitland and Miss McGuire when we return to the office on Monday morning? And for another—'

'Tuesday morning,' Marcus corrected. 'We aren't leaving until Monday afternoon,' he explained as she looked at him enquiringly.

So now, attracted to him as she was, she had three torturous days in his company instead of two!

Great!

'But you're right about the Miss McGuire bit,' Marcus continued thoughtfully. 'Looking at you now, I'm not sure I will ever be able to think of you in that guise ever again!'

Hadn't she tried to tell him that—?

'Or for you to return to that coolly efficient role, either,' he said pointedly.

Kit winced as she inwardly acknowledged that her change in appearance had also resulted in certain sub-tle—and some not so subtle!—differences in her per-sonality. Dressed in her casual clothes, her hair loose, and no heavy-framed glasses, she certainly felt, and behaved, differently from the coolly capable Miss McGuire!

'All in all—Kit,' he paused briefly before deliber-ately using her first name, 'I have a feeling that being away on business with you is going to be altogether a completely different experience to going away with Lewis!'

That was what she was afraid of!

Marcus glanced at her, chuckling huskily as he saw the woebegone expression on her face. 'Cheer up, Kit,' he encouraged. 'What's the worst that could happen?'

Attracted to him as she was, feeling about him the way that she did, she would rather not think about that, either!

'After all,' Marcus went on lightly, completely re-laxed now as he drove effortlessly along the country roads, 'you're going to be chaperoned by several other guests. And don't forget, my taste runs to dumb blondes.'

She gave a pained groan. 'I wish that I had never made that remark!'

Marcus was grinning, obviously enjoying her dis-comfort now. 'Well, it's a sure fact you aren't blonde.' He gave her hair an admiring glance. 'And I can per-sonally vouch for the fact that you aren't dumb, either!'

She gave a heavy sigh. 'Mr Maitland—'

'Marcus,' he reminded her firmly. 'Is Kit short for something else?' he mused. 'Kitty or Kathryn, something like that?'

'It's short for Kit,' she told him woodenly. 'Plain and simple Kit.'

'Okay.' He shrugged broad shoulders. 'You were going to say something before we got into this discussion about names…?'

'Before *you* got into the discussion about names,' she corrected flatly. 'And I was just going to apologize—' once again! '—for my remarks about your personal life. They were rude, and intrusive, and altogether—'

'True,' he finished happily. 'But I'm sure it isn't too late for my tastes to change—to tall, outspoken redheads, for instance.'

Kit was almost afraid to look at him now, sure he was just teasing her to get his own back for her earlier remarks—but at the same time she wasn't sure of any such thing!

It was difficult to tell what he was thinking from the blandness of his expression. Deliberately so? Probably, she acknowledged heavily. One thing she had learnt over the last couple of days: Marcus had a wicked sense of humour when he chose to exert it.

'Very funny,' she scorned, choosing to err on the side of caution. 'Do you have any idea who any of the other guests will be this weekend?' She deliberately changed the subject onto something less personal. And disturbing!

'The usual hangers-on and social bores a man like Desmond Hayes attracts, I suppose. Never mind, Kit, we'll have each other for company.'

Now she knew he was deliberately teasing her. Because he knew she found him attractive? Because he had guessed that, against all the warnings, she had fallen into the trap of being half in love with him? That would be just too awful! Well, in this case, lack of interest was the best form of defence...

'How nice.' She made her reply deliberately saccharine-sweet.

Marcus gave an appreciative laugh. 'Well, I can assure you, Kit, *I'm* certainly not expecting to be bored!'

While he kept teasing her like this, no, she didn't expect that he would be...

She gave a weary yawn. 'I'm feeling rather tired. Would you mind if I had a short nap before we arrive?' Not waiting for his reply, she settled herself down in her seat and closed her eyes.

Shutting out his image along with it.

But not her full awareness of him. Of the lean strength of his hands as he drove with such easy assurance. Or, the sprinkling of dark hair that ran the length of his arms. And further. The determination of his jaw. The full sensuality of his lips. The dark blue of his eyes. The way those eyes crinkled at the corners when he smiled or laughed. The potent, slightly elusive smell of his aftershave.

Face it, Kit, she told herself derisively; you stand about as much chance of relaxing around Marcus Maitland, of really going to sleep, as you do sitting next to a tiger poised to spring!

But that didn't stop her giving every appearance of dozing during the rest of the journey, only making a pretence of waking as Marcus touched her arm lightly and told her that they had arrived.

'You had a good nap,' he told her admiringly as he brought the Jaguar to a stop on the gravel driveway in front of what looked like once having been a stately home. Huge pillars supported its entranceway, the stonework old and mellowed. Noise seemed to flow from every open window as the two of them stepped out onto the gravel driveway, where there were a dozen or so other cars already parked outside.

'''Come and spend a peaceful weekend in the country'' was how Desmond described it to me!' Marcus gave a hint of his distaste for the loud music and chatter as he moved to get their bags from the boot of the car.

Although not normally one for crowds of people on a superficial basis, Kit found herself smiling, quite happy to make this weekend the exception; the more people there were around them, the less likely she was to be so aware of Marcus. Or to spend too much time alone with him.

'It sounds like fun,' she responded lightly.

Marcus gave a disgusted snort, leading the way up the stone steps that fronted the house. Its massive front door was thrown open and the large entrance hall inside was filled with what looked like dozens of people.

'Are you sure you have the right weekend?' Kit questioned of Marcus.

'I'm sure,' he replied grimly. 'You—'

'Kit? Hey, Kit, is that really you?' called out a familiar voice.

A voice that made her freeze in her tracks and caused the smile to fade from her lips as she looked frantically around the entrance hall for its source.

And then she saw him, making his way purposefully

towards her, a smile of amused recognition on his over-confident, too-handsome face.

Mike Reynolds.

Her ex-boss from hell.

But he wasn't the sole reason her cheeks paled and her breathing seemed to stop. There was also another person whom she could see standing a short distance behind Mike Reynolds. Someone Kit wanted to see even less than she did Mike!

Catherine Grainger...

CHAPTER FOUR

K<small>IT</small> was so stunned that she stood totally immobile as Mike Reynolds took her in his arms and gave her a bear hug.

It was as if he had totally forgotten that the last time the two of them had met she had told him exactly what he could do with his job—and his sexual harassment!

But Kit hadn't forgotten, stiffening in his arms and trying to push him away, panic setting in as she wished herself anywhere but here. Mike Reynolds was bad enough, but she could handle him. She just hadn't been prepared for that other, much more disturbing guest.

Mike stepped back, his hands gripping the tops of her arms as he held her in front of him. 'You're looking good, kid,' he said, his bold blue gaze moving slowly down the length of her body.

Kit's mouth tightened at his familiarity, her eyes glowing deeply grey as she glared at him. 'It's a pity—'

'—that we haven't seen each other for so long,' he completed smoothly.

She had been going to say something much more insulting! Which was totally unlike her. But after the shock she had just received, politeness—especially to Mike Reynolds!—was the last thing on her mind.

Mike nodded appreciatively, apparently completely impervious to her less-than-enthusiastic response as his arm slid lightly across her shoulders as he moved to stand next to her. 'Aren't you going to introduce me to your friend, Kit?' he prompted lightly as he looked curiously at Marcus.

Marcus!

It was testament to the shock she had received in the last few moments that she had completely forgotten Marcus had entered the house with her. In fact, she had completely forgotten everything else but that disturbing female presence standing only metres away from her!

She shrugged off the arm Mike had draped about her shoulders, moving deliberately away from him to stand next to Marcus. She shot a glance at her boss; he was watching her and Mike, his expression unreadable, his gaze hooded.

'Yes, do introduce us, Kit,' he encouraged now in a voice that sounded as if it came after walking over broken glass.

Kit winced at the sound of it, knowing that the last thing she wanted to do was introduce these two men. Yet it seemed that was the one thing she was going to have to do if she was going to escape from this hallway any time soon. And she most certainly was going to have to escape, to find somewhere she could be on her own for a while, if only to give herself time to decide what she should do next.

Because she couldn't stay on here. Not now.

'Marcus Maitland. Mike Reynolds,' she introduced stiffly, seriously wondering if this weekend could get any worse than it already was. Not only Mike Reynolds, of all people, but—

'Marcus! Darling…!' suddenly greeted an all-too-familiar voice.

It just had, Kit acknowledged with an inward groan.

Andrea Revel's heady perfume enveloped them all as she moved into their group and stood on tiptoe to kiss Marcus lingeringly on the lips.

'And Kit, too.' Andrea turned to her, the light of triumph in those cat-green eyes before she gave Kit the merest peck on the cheek. 'How nice,' she added with dismissive insincerity before turning back to Marcus. 'Derek Boyes was kind enough to invite me to come with him this weekend,' she told him with glee as she linked her arm companionably with his.

Kit looked at Marcus beneath lowered lids, but it was impossible to tell from his enigmatic expression just how he was taking that particular piece of news. Although he had to feel something; after all—despite Marcus's claim that the relationship was over—he and Andrea had been something of an item for at least the last couple of months.

'How nice,' he finally answered with the same insincerity Andrea had used towards Kit a few minutes ago.

Causing Kit to look at him with a new appreciation; perhaps he wasn't as blind to this woman's bitchiness as she had thought that he was…?

'Well, if the two of you will excuse us…?' He deftly removed his arm from Andrea's clinging grasp as he bent to pick up his and Kit's cases. 'Kit and I have only just arrived, so I think it might be appropriate if we find our host and say hello, don't you?' Without waiting for a response from either Mike Reynolds or Andrea, he motioned Kit with an urgent inclination of his head to move further into the house.

Further into the lion's den, as far as Kit was concerned. This weekend was just going from bad to

worse. And she had thought the only thing she would
have to worry about during the next couple of days
was keeping her feelings towards Marcus hidden from
him!

A glance at his face as they walked away from the
other couple was enough to tell Kit that he wasn't quite
as calm as he wanted to appear: his mouth was set
grimly, his eyes narrowed to icy blue slits.

'Stop looking so worried, Kit,' he bit out between
clenched teeth. 'I'm not the type to make a scene.'

She hadn't for a moment thought that he was—it was
that he had just thought about making one that bothered
her!

But perhaps the fact that Andrea was here with another man had made him realise he didn't want the
woman out of his life, after all? What other possible
reason could there be for him making a scene...?

But Marcus's attention seemed to become distracted
as he looked around them, that frownline back between
his eyes. 'There's something odd going on here,' he
muttered harshly.

Surely he hadn't just noticed! Her ex-boss was here,
someone she had hoped never to see again, and the
current woman in his life was here with another man,
and as for—

'Look around you, Kit,' he said.

She gave him a startled look. 'Look—?'

'Just look,' Marcus encouraged gruffly.

Kit looked, seeing twenty or so other guests: all of
the men looked rich and confident, the women beautiful and glamorous.

But when she looked closer, at individuals, she realised that she recognized quite a number of the men,

that several of them had either met with Marcus on business, or she had actually seen their photographs—including Mike Reynolds's!—in the business newspapers in connection with one successful deal or another.

'Exactly,' Marcus pronounced as he saw the dawning realisation on her face. 'It seems I'm not the only one to have heard the rumours. Or that Desmond isn't averse to actually using those rumours to his own advantage,' he added knowingly.

Kit instantly saw what he meant by that remark. Bring together a group of a dozen businessmen, supposedly on a social basis, but with the real object of picking up a bargain on a business deal—like sharks circling one of their own injured species!—and the price on those deals was sure to go higher than if business had been done with those individuals on a private basis.

She gave a rueful smile. 'He could even have started them.'

Marcus turned to give her an admiring look. 'You're turning out to be amazingly astute, Kit,' he said appreciatively.

She felt the blush in her cheeks at this unexpected compliment. 'It was just a guess,' she admitted. 'I could be completely wrong.'

He gave her a teasing smile. 'I'm not sure that—well, well, well,' he said consideringly as something over her left shoulder caught and held his attention, his expression once again enigmatic.

Kit stiffened. 'What is it?' she asked as he continued to look at something—or someone!—behind her.

'Hmm?' he murmured distractedly. 'Let's go and say hello to our esteemed host, shall we?' He didn't wait for her reply before grasping her arm with his free hand and directing her across the hallway.

Kit almost came to a full stop again as she saw their host chatting amiably with a number of people, easily recognizing several of them; Mike Reynolds had joined them, since she and Marcus had left him a couple of minutes ago.

Marcus turned to give her a curious glance as he sensed her reluctance to join the group. 'How about we have a little chat about—your friend, later, hmm?' he suggested.

She gave him a sharp look before replying, 'Mike Reynolds is no friend of mine!'

'I already gathered that,' Marcus replied. 'But I have a feeling that he was once,' he added speculatively.

'No way!' Kit denied heatedly. 'Mike Reynolds is nothing but a—'

'Later, Kit,' Marcus advised tersely as they reached their host. 'And don't forget what I told you: observe and listen.' He turned a socially bright smile on Desmond Hayes. 'Quite a crowd you have here, Desmond,' he greeted the other man jovially, releasing Kit's arm to shake the other man's hand.

'Marcus!' The other man's face lit with recognition. 'So glad you could make it,' he welcomed with the smooth charm for which he was renowned. He was a tall, attractive man in his late fifties, his dark hair sprinkled with silver, his lined face handsome, his smiling blue eyes sharply intelligent.

Kit stood slightly behind the two men as they greeted each other, trying to make herself as inconspicuous as possible. 'Observe and listen,' Marcus had told her—when all she really wanted to do was blend in with the velvet-embossed wallpaper, disappear into it if that were at all possible!

How much longer was this torture to go on before she could escape to the bedroom she had been allocated and actually give herself time to think—and breathe? Because she was sure she had all but stopped doing the latter a good five minutes ago!

'And this is Kit. Kit…?' Marcus called sharply, having turned to introduce her only to find her lurking behind him.

She moistened dry lips, keeping her gaze down on the carpeted floor as she held out her hand to the other man. 'Mr Hayes,' she greeted shyly.

'Desmond, please,' the older man encouraged with warm invitation, holding onto her hand to pull her slightly forward as she would have released it. 'And just where has Marcus been hiding you?' he queried.

Kit swallowed, still not looking up, but very much aware that the group around them had grown silent now as they listened to the exchange. Exchange? It could hardly be called that when Desmond Hayes was the one doing all the talking! In a flirtatious way he had. And, to add to her confusion, he still hadn't released her hand!

She moistened her lips once again. 'I—'

'Careful, Desmond,' Marcus told the other man with lazy derision, his arm moving casually about Kit's shoulders as he did so.

'Private property, eh, Marcus?' the older man said regretfully.

Kit found this whole conversation distasteful—and attention-drawing. Which was what she most certainly didn't want at this particular moment!

'Something like that,' Marcus returned noncommittally.

'Can I offer the two of you glasses of champagne?' Without waiting for their answer, Desmond Hayes plucked two flutes off the tray that a passing waiter was carrying.

Kit accepted the glass he held out to her, taking a much-needed sip of the bubbly liquid it contained. Getting drunk certainly wouldn't help this situation, but hopefully she would become too numb to care!

Marcus held up the two bags he was carrying. 'Are you going to tell us where the two of us are to sleep so that I can get rid of these, or do we just go upstairs and take our pick of bedrooms?' he prompted.

'I'll have Forbes take your luggage upstairs,' Desmond Hayes murmured apologetically, giving Kit's hand one last familiar squeeze before releasing it to turn and signal to the butler standing unobtrusively down the hallway. The elderly man immediately came over to relieve Marcus of the two bags.

Not that Kit was taking too much notice of these proceedings, still caught up in Marcus's last comment, especially the part about, 'where the two of us are to sleep'!

Surely Marcus wasn't expecting them to share a bedroom? That would be taking her supposed role as the current woman in his life a little too far. In fact, as far as she was concerned, much too far!

'Catherine,' Marcus was greeting lightly now as their host disappeared to instruct Forbes on where to put their luggage, turning to smile coolly at the woman who stood slightly apart from the other guests.

Almost as if, like Kit, she were trying to remain

unobtrusive. And yet Kit knew that couldn't be true. It was more likely that the older woman was watching them all with the contemptuous amusement for which she was so well known.

The woman's height only added to her imperiousness, her smooth, shoulder-length hair completely without adornment, or any pretence of hiding its silver colour, confirming her sixty-seven years, though her figure was still youthfully slim in the plain black dress she wore, and the unlined beauty of her face dominated by hard silver-grey eyes.

Kit had never actually met her before, and yet she would have known her anywhere.

Catherine Grainger.

Marcus's arch business enemy...

But also the very, very last person of whom Kit wanted to be within one hundred miles!

CHAPTER FIVE

'WILL you stop pacing up and down like that?' Marcus said as he lay back on the bed watching her. 'I feel exhausted just watching you!'

Kit spared him an annoyed glance, but didn't hesitate in her pacing. This whole situation was intolerable, and all he could do was lie there looking—looking—utterly desirable!

His dark hair was ruffled, his eyes sleepily sensual— and the fact that he was completely relaxed as he lay on the bed certainly didn't help to allay that impression!

'Look on the bright side, Kit—'

'Is there one?' she groaned, moving to stand next to the bed. 'And will you please get up?' she demanded. 'This is where I have to sleep tonight.' Something that was going to be virtually impossible for her to do now she had the image of this man lying back on her pillow!

'Sorry!' Marcus sat up slowly, eyeing her with amusement. 'But surely that is the bright side?' he encouraged. 'At least we have adjoining bedrooms rather than having to share one.'

Oh, yes, that was really comforting! The connecting door between the two bedrooms stood wide open at the moment, with no key on either side to lock it even when it was closed. Kit knew this, for she had already looked for one!

The half an hour or so of torture Marcus had spent

downstairs socializing with the other weekend guests before coming up to change for dinner was nothing compared to finding that they had been given connecting bedrooms.

'Personally, I think it was pretty decent of Desmond not to have just assumed that we—well, that we—'

'Are lovers?' Kit finished forcefully, way beyond being reasoned with.

Marcus shrugged. 'Well, you have to appreciate that it's good of him, given the circumstances, and the amount of other people here for the weekend. After all, this isn't a hotel; I could hardly phone on ahead and book two single rooms!'

She didn't have to give Desmond Hayes anything. Or Marcus Maitland, either, for that matter!

'You wouldn't have done it anyway—I would!' She sighed, her nerve endings feeling so frayed she wanted to scream.

The hour since they had arrived at Desmond Hayes's home had been filled with one shock after another, so much so that all Kit wanted to do right now was lock herself in the *en suite* bathroom and stay there until it was all over. She certainly wasn't in the mood to be teased and cajoled!

She glared at Marcus, her hands clenched at her sides, so agitated that she felt as if she wanted to hit someone, if not physically then verbally would do. 'Is this the usual practice when you're away with your PA? Was that the reason that Angie Dwyer told me about you, the reason she decided to leave? Did she object to—?'

'Careful, Kit,' Marcus cut in with quiet intensity, his eyes narrowed. 'I may be feeling pretty mellow at the moment, but I would advise you not to forget exactly what the two of us are doing here.'

She breathed deeply. 'That's the problem; I'm no longer sure what I'm doing here. If this really is a working weekend, then that's okay. But if you expect me to—to—' she made an agitated gesture towards the rumpled bed that he still sat on '—then I'm afraid you're going to be sadly disappointed, because I—'

'Stop right there,' he commanded harshly, standing up so abruptly that Kit took an involuntary step backwards. He gave a humourless smile as he saw the movement. 'To put the record straight, the reason Angie Dwyer decided to leave had nothing to do with my behaviour—and everything to do with her own!' He grimaced. 'To be ungentlemanly about it—'

'Oh, do!' Kit invited agitatedly.

He gave her a warning look. 'To be ungentlemanly about it,' he repeated tautly, 'Angie was the one who decided our relationship could be a little more—intimate, shall we say? I don't get involved with employees. For goodness' sake, Kit,' he implored as she still looked unconvinced. 'Need I remind you that until a couple of hours ago you looked as desirable as someone's maiden aunt. I certainly didn't give you the job because of the way you looked!'

Of course he hadn't, she realised self-disgustedly. She was just so upset by whom she was expected to spend this weekend with that she had gone completely off on a tangent. As if Marcus would ever find her attractive, even without the severe hairstyle and glasses, when there were women like Andrea Revel falling all over him.

And that was something else...!

'Okay,' she dismissed tautly. 'I suggest we forget about that side of things for the moment.'

Especially as she had been completely wrong in her conclusions about his relationship with Angie Dwyer. She should have known from her conversation with Angie that she'd had some sort of chip on her shoulder about Marcus. From the other woman's catty remarks about his private life, namely the women who populated it, perhaps it should have been obvious what that chip had been.

'Big of you,' he muttered.

Her eyes glowed deeply grey. 'You have no idea how big.' She sighed, remembering only too well those awful months she had spent working for Mike Reynolds. 'But what are you going to do about Andrea Revel?' she challenged.

Marcus raised dark brows. 'Do about her?'

Kit gave him a frowning glance. 'As in her being here this weekend at all.'

'But she's not here with me, is she?' he reasoned. 'You are.'

'Yes, but—but—'

'We're back to that broken record again. The fact that Andrea is here has absolutely nothing to do with me,' he told her clearly. 'She came with Derek Boyes; she's his problem.'

Kit couldn't agree with him, on either statement; he and Andrea had ended their relationship because he had told her he was bringing Kit instead of her, and if Andrea was anyone's problem, then she was definitely Marcus's!

'Mr Maitland—'

'I thought we had agreed that, for this weekend at

least, it's to be Marcus and Kit?' he reminded her dryly.

'But that's my whole point!' she said frustratedly. 'Andrea—Miss Revel—knows that the two of us aren't a couple.'

'Does she?' He looked at her with steady blue eyes.

Kit blinked. 'Doesn't she?'

He shrugged. 'A little hard to tell, wouldn't you say, considering the changes in your appearance, and the fact that we're sharing a suite?'

'Yes, but—okay, let's just forget the broken-record remarks,' she offered. 'Until yesterday the two of you were—well, you were!' she accused.

'And now we're not,' he dismissed unconcernedly. 'Life moves on very fast sometimes, doesn't it? And at other times…' he stood up, moving purposefully towards her '…it moves very slowly…' Before Kit even had time to gauge what he was doing, his head lowered and his mouth claimed hers.

There was no thought of denial on her part as she melted into his hardness, her lips parting beneath his.

She had longed for this all those months of working beside Marcus, had lain awake at nights wondering what it would be like to be kissed by him. And now she knew.

It was wonderful!

His arms moved about the slenderness of her waist as he moulded her body against his, his tongue moving in exploration of the sensuous warmth of her bottom lip, her groan of capitulation all the encouragement he needed to deepen the kiss.

Kit felt like liquid fire in his arms, her body pressed

against his, groaning low in her throat as she felt the caress of his hand against the curve of her breast.

Quite what would have happened next, Kit had no idea, if a door banging noisily shut further down the corridor hadn't made her start back guiltily to stare up at Marcus with disbelieving eyes.

His expression was unreadable, his blue eyes shuttered as he looked back at her.

Kit swallowed hard, her tongue moving to moisten her lips as she searched for something to say. What could she say? Except the obvious!

'Didn't you just violate your own rule where employees are concerned?' she ventured—desperately hoping to divert his attention from the fact that she had very definitely responded to him!

His mouth quirked. 'I read somewhere once that "rules are made for the guidance of wise men and the blind obedience of fools"!'

Kit raised auburn brows. 'And which are you?'

'At this moment? Anybody's guess!'

She couldn't help it—she laughed. A light, relieved laugh that seemed to release some of the tension that had surrounded them.

Marcus's smile was sheepish as he ran a hand through the dark thickness of his hair. 'I apologize, Kit. I suppose it's no good asking you to forget it ever happened?'

Well…she could try. But did she really want to? As regards the two of them continuing to work together, she knew that she had to, but as Kit McGuire…she had enjoyed the kiss too much to ever really want to forget it had happened.

'We could try,' she answered as noncommittally as

she could, her gaze not quite meeting his now. 'But for the moment,' she added briskly, 'shouldn't we be changing for dinner?'

Marcus sighed heavily. 'That was the plan.'

'Well…?' she prompted as he made no effort to go to the adjoining bedroom.

He gave a perplexed frown as he looked at her. 'Incredible!' he exclaimed. 'And after my self-righteous claim of never becoming involved with my employees…'

'I promise not to tell anyone if you don't!' Kit's cheeks burned with embarrassment.

'Kit—'

'I really do need to change,' she reminded him firmly before turning away.

But she could sense his presence in the room behind her for several more long seconds before he moved away, the adjoining door closing softly behind him and telling her when she was at last alone.

What had they done?

What had she done?

Her obvious course of action should have been to have stopped the kiss before it had even started. If she hadn't been enjoying it so much she might just have done that!

But it had been wonderful. All she had ever thought kissing Marcus would be. And she had spent quite a few hours during the last six months wondering exactly that.

Besides, the kiss had certainly taken Marcus's mind off discussing her 'friend', Mike Reynolds!

She paused from unpacking the black dress she intended wearing this evening. Mike Reynolds, of all people. And he'd had the cheek to greet her as if the two of them hadn't parted on such bad terms seven months ago!

And just how much longer was she going to delay thinking of that other—even less welcome!—guest? Kit asked herself candidly.

The rest of her life, she could have hoped. But it was no good trying to deny the fact that Catherine Grainger was also a weekend guest here.

But would the lady have a clue as to who Kit was? If she did, Kit knew only too well that the other woman wouldn't be interested.

Kit's mouth tightened. Irrational though it was, how she disliked Ms Grainger! Her arrogance. Her coldness. Just her complete air of superiority.

But what would Marcus say if he were to know Kit's secret? Especially since there seemed to be a security leak in his company where Catherine Grainger was concerned... He could think it very odd that Kit hadn't told him the truth in the first place. But other than telling Marcus everything—something she had no intention of doing unless forced—there was no way she could explain away her knowledge of the older woman. She would just have to keep hoping—and praying!—that Catherine never guessed the truth.

If only she could avoid so much as talking to Catherine for the brief time they were here!

Something she didn't look like doing when the first person she saw as she came down the stairs twenty minutes later was—Catherine Grainger, who was standing in the entrance hall talking on her mobile telephone.

Kit had knocked on the adjoining door between

Marcus's room and her own a few minutes earlier, only to find that he had just come out of the shower, wearing nothing but a towel wrapped about his waist.

After a first glance Kit's eyes had remained fixed on the picture on the wall behind him, wings of colour burning in her cheeks. 'And they say women take a long time to get ready!' she joked weakly.

'I was delayed by a telephone call,' he came back swiftly.

Kit glanced at him. 'Andrea?'

He gave an acknowledging inclination of his head. 'How very astute of you!'

'Not really,' she assured him; Marcus might have calmly dismissed Andrea's presence here as being none of his business, but it was a certainty that Andrea, having had time to think about the abrupt end of her relationship with him, wasn't going to do the same where he was concerned. 'I'll wait for you downstairs, shall I?'

'Unless you want to sit down and wait while I get dressed?' he taunted, dark brows raised in invitation.

'No, thank you,' Kit came back stiffly, already turning towards the door as she heard him chuckle under his breath.

Which accounted for why she was completely on her own now as she descended the stairs to meet Catherine Grainger, the only other person in the huge entrance hall...

CHAPTER SIX

'I DON'T believe we were introduced earlier…?'

Kit froze two steps from the bottom of the staircase as Catherine spoke to her. No, they hadn't been introduced, deliberately so, as far as Kit was concerned; she was determined to avoid Catherine Grainger as much as was possible.

'Have the two of us met before…?' Puzzlement edged the older woman's clipped tones as she spoke again.

Kit's chin rose and she looked down at the other woman, schooling her features into polite disinterest. 'I'm sure not,' she replied, only the whitening of her knuckles as she tightly gripped the banister beside her demonstrating that she wasn't quite as composed as she might appear.

There had been a time in her life when she had imagined a moment like this, when she and Catherine Grainger would come face to face. But that had been when she was still young enough to believe in fairness and justice. Reality was something else entirely.

Catherine was so tall and slim that she looked elegant in whatever she wore, tonight a dress of sparkling midnight blue. Her silver hair lightly touched her bare shoulders, and her throat sported a simple necklace of sapphire and diamonds—her only jewellery.

One of those diamond necklaces that Marcus had wanted to strangle her with only yesterday!

But despite the elegance of her dress, the understated simplicity of the jewellery, everything about this woman spoke of wealth and power.

'You seem familiar somehow,' Catherine persisted, her silver-grey gaze focused assessingly on Kit now.

Kit's own black dress was nowhere near as expensively tailored as Catherine's, and her only jewellery was a small gold locket suspended between her breasts by a delicate gold chain.

What would Catherine Grainger have to say if she could see the two people photographed inside that locket?

Not a lot, Kit sadly hazarded a guess.

'Doubtful,' she answered Catherine, finishing her descent of the stairs, standing only feet away from her now.

Catherine's gaze remained on her. 'You arrived with Marcus Maitland, didn't you?' she probed.

Kit smiled slightly at the slight edge in Catherine's voice. 'I did,' she confirmed, inwardly pleased to be able to make that claim; the obvious dislike between this lady and Marcus was one sure way to keep her, and her curiosity, at bay!

Catherine's mouth curved derisively. 'No accounting for taste, I suppose,' she drawled scathingly.

Kit stiffened. 'Please don't let me keep you from the other guests,' she replied, hearing the distinctive murmur of voices coming from a double-doored room to their right.

'You aren't,' the other woman countered. 'In fact—'

'There you are, Kit!' Marcus greeted from the top of the stairs, both women turning to look at him as he descended.

Marcus looked devastatingly attractive in a black dinner suit and snowy white shirt, more so than Kit had ever seen him before.

Catherine Grainger's expression remained impassive, confirming that there was no love lost between the two of them.

'Catherine,' Marcus greeted smoothly as he reached the hallway, his hand moving possessively on the slenderness of Kit's waist.

Kit turned to him, groaning inwardly as she saw the hard glitter in his eyes.

'Marcus,' Catherine returned dryly. 'Your—young friend, and I were just keeping each other company while she waited for you to come downstairs.'

'Really?' he drawled sceptically. 'Well, I'm obviously here now, so please don't let us delay you any further.' He looked at the older woman challengingly.

A challenge she was only too pleased to meet, mocking humour to her smile now. 'I'm in no hurry.' She shrugged her elegant shoulders. 'Perhaps the three of us could go to the library and have a quiet drink togeth—'

'I wondered what was keeping you, Catherine,' Desmond Hayes called out reprovingly after flinging open the double doors to the sitting-room to find the three of them standing there. 'Now I see that it was Marcus—' he strolled over to join them '—and his charming companion, Kit,' he added with obvious intent, his eyes flirting shamelessly as he took in her appearance.

Kit winced as Marcus's grip on her waist tightened; was she going to do anything right at all this evening?

She knew from Marcus's response to finding her

downstairs with Catherine that he wasn't pleased to see them together—well, he could join the club, because Kit wasn't pleased about it either! But he had no right at all to be annoyed with her because Desmond Hayes kept flirting with her—she certainly wasn't encouraging the man!

'Kit…' Catherine repeated consideringly, once again eyeing Kit speculatively. 'Would that be short for—?'

'It would be short for nothing,' Kit cut in firmly. 'And I'm sure the three of us have already delayed dinner for long enough,' she finished with a pointed smile in Desmond Hayes's direction.

'You two go ahead,' Marcus suggested tautly.

'If you're sure,' Desmond Hayes accepted as he tucked Catherine's hand snugly into the crook of his arm.

'I'm sure,' Marcus confirmed. 'Kit and I will join you in a few moments.' His grip on her waist held her back now as the other couple moved towards the noisy sitting-room.

Kit should have felt relieved at their departure—and she did feel a certain amount of tension ease out of her—but the anger she could still feel emanating from Marcus as he watched Catherine and Desmond was enough to tell her he was far from finished talking to her. In fact, he probably hadn't even started yet.

He moved away from her as soon as the sitting-room doors closed, looking down at her with accusing eyes. 'How long have you known Catherine Grainger?'

Kit felt her cheeks pale. 'I—but I don't know her!' she claimed dazedly.

His mouth twisted humourlessly. 'The two of you

looked friendly enough when I came downstairs a few minutes ago.'

Kit scowled as she gathered her wits. 'How can you say that? We had barely got past the civilities when you appeared—'

Marcus eyed her scathingly. 'Kit, I had been watching the two of you for several minutes before making my presence known.'

Her eyes widened. 'You were spying on us?' she realised incredulously.

'Of course not,' he dismissed irritably. 'I was merely on my way downstairs when I—'

'Saw the two of us talking together and decided to listen in!' Kit finished disgustedly, just thankful that he couldn't possibly have heard anything in the least damning—simply because there hadn't been anything like that for him to hear!

Marcus drew in a deep, controlling breath. 'Kit, are you aware of the—rivalry, between Maitland Enterprises and Grainger International?

'And the fact that they seem to be stealing the march on us lately with several business deals?'

'Well, of course I'm aware of it. I'm your PA—now just a minute.' She drew herself up to her current full height of six feet—in the two-inch-high-heeled shoes she was wearing—and was almost able to meet Marcus eye to eye. 'Exactly what are you implying?'

'I've suggested to Lewis that there may be some connection between the last three deals that Grainger International have stolen from under our noses.'

'Yes?' she prompted slowly, remembering all too well Lewis Grant's remarks on the subject on Thursday. And the implication behind them. 'When you said lately just now, did you really mean to say in the last six months?' she pressed resentfully. 'The exact amount of time I've been working for you?'

'Calm down, Kit.' Marcus sighed. 'I didn't mean to imply—'

'Oh, yes, you did!' Kit bit out indignantly. 'How dare you? How dare you even think such a thing about me and that—that woman?' she finished for want of something better to say.

The things he was implying about her, that she might possibly have leaked information to Catherine Grainger—presumably, he thought, for some monetary reward to herself?—would be laughable if they weren't so insulting!

'For your information, I wouldn't offer to help that woman—in any way—if she and I were the last two people on the planet!' Kit was breathing so hard in her agitation that her creamy breasts were clearly heaving beneath the low neckline of her dress.

Not that she was too concerned about that, realising as she saw the sudden change in Marcus's expression that she had said too much; Marcus was far too intelligent a man to believe she could possibly have come to that conclusion about Catherine Grainger after only five minutes' acquaintance!

Which she obviously hadn't. No, her knowledge of Catherine went back much further than that. Too far back to even give Marcus a hint at the reason she felt the way she did.

She made a dismissive movement of her hand. 'What I meant to say was—'

'I believe you made yourself more than clear, Kit,' Marcus assured her dryly. 'And I apologize if my remarks just now were less than—well, trusting.' He grimaced. 'All I'm saying is that I'm inclined to think the only explanation for those three lost deals is that there is someone in my employ who is revealing details of my business interests to Grainger International. But just because you and Catherine were talking together just now is really no reason for me to think that you—'

'That I'm the disloyal employee,' Kit completed tautly, having already known—and dreaded—the connection he could make concerning her and Catherine Grainger. 'Maybe you should try looking a little closer to home for your leak?' she suggested, still smarting from the fact that he might have thought it could have been her.

He blinked. 'Such as where?'

Kit gave him a smile of completely insincere sweetness. 'Did it ever occur to you that maybe you talk in your sleep?'

Marcus looked momentarily stunned by the suggestion. But then his good humour, which had been such a welcome surprise to Kit the last few days, took over, and a wry smile started to curve his lips. 'I think maybe I deserved that,' he acknowledged.

She gave an accepting inclination of her head. 'I think maybe you did.'

'Hmm,' he murmured ruefully, still smiling. 'Am I forgiven?' His expression was cajoling.

She was still annoyed with him, but at the same time knew how ludicrous were his suspicions that she could have betrayed him to Catherine Grainger. But Marcus couldn't know that. And she would rather it remained that way.

'You are,' she returned lightly.

'In that case—' he reached out to take a courteous hold of her arm '—shall we join the others, Miss McGuire?'

'Certainly, Mr Maitland,' she instantly accepted, knowing that if he had overstepped a line where she was concerned, then she had certainly done the same thing to him with her inference about pillow talk with women like Andrea Revel—and got away with it, thank goodness!

She had no idea what had prompted her to make that completely personal remark, except that it had disturbed her to have him accuse her of somehow being in cahoots with Catherine Grainger, of all people. She would rather ally herself to a rattlesnake!

'But don't be under the misapprehension,' Marcus murmured close to her ear as they entered the noisy sitting-room, 'that because I made a mistake about Catherine Grainger, I've forgotten our need to discuss your—acquaintance, with Mike Reynolds.'

Kit turned sharply, the high colour back in her cheeks. 'I don't feel such a need!' she assured him quickly.

He raised dark brows at her vehemence. 'Like that, is it?'

'Exactly like that!' If she never saw Mike Reynolds again it would be too soon!

Marcus gave her a considering look. 'There really is a lot more to you than meets the eye, Kit McGuire—'

'I thought that for this weekend it was to be Marcus and Kit?' she reminded him, preferring not to have her surname bandied. Especially in Catherine Grainger's hearing...

'Oh, it is,' he replied. 'Have I told you yet this evening how beautiful you look?'

If anything that colour in her cheeks deepened. 'There's no need to keep up the pretence when we're on our own,' she informed him awkwardly.

'It's not pretence,' he assured her softly, blue eyes laughing warmly as she gave him a puzzled look. 'You really are a very beautiful woman, Kit,' he told her seriously. 'I had absolutely no idea.'

'Perhaps it might be better if we left it that way,' she said stiffly.

'Too late,' he responded. 'I think simply coming in to the office might be a pleasure in future!'

Kit didn't feel the same enthusiasm, not if it was based on the fact that he now found her an attractive woman. Considering the short amount of time his interest in a specific woman usually lasted, that could mean that her days as his PA were numbered...

'Especially...' he looked at her intently '...if you really have forgiven me for my remarks of a few minutes ago?'

Kit gave an abrupt nod of her head. 'I said I had.'

Marcus grimaced. 'It's been my experience that women don't always mean what they say.'

'Well, this one does!' she assured him firmly.

Oh, she had forgiven him. Of course she had. But she wouldn't forget. Couldn't forget.

Because if Marcus knew the truth about her acquaintance with Catherine Grainger, she was sure he wouldn't have Kit anywhere near him, let alone working in his office!

CHAPTER SEVEN

'I THOUGHT the man was never going to leave your side!' Mike Reynolds complained as he joined Kit beside the buffet table and a mouth-watering array of desserts.

Because of the amount of people staying at the house this weekend dinner had necessarily been a full buffet affair, which actually suited Kit much better than being seated formally at a dinner table and stuck between two men she would probably rather not spend the time of day—or evening!—with.

Which pretty much covered most of the men here this weekend. With the exception of those wealthy businessmen—and women!—Kit had noted earlier, she had so far found them exactly as Marcus had earlier described them, a lot of 'hangers-on and social bores'. And Mike Reynolds came even further down the social list as far as she was concerned!

'Marcus will be back in a few minutes,' she informed Mike frostily, her expression one of utter contempt as she looked unflinchingly into his too-handsome face. 'He's just slipped upstairs to collect some cigars he brought with him for our host.'

'So I noticed,' Mike responded comfortably, as usual not affected by her obvious dislike. 'I also noticed Andrea Revel slipping out to join him a few seconds later,' he added. 'So if I were you, I wouldn't count on your boyfriend being back any time soon!'

Kit tried very hard not to show her surprise—and chagrin—at being told that Andrea was upstairs with Marcus. Not that she really was that surprised that Andrea hadn't given up on Marcus; she had been extremely visible during the last hour or so as they had all stood or sat around eating their sumptuous dinner, her loud laughter ringing out often at something her companion—presumably Derek Boyes—had said to her.

Not that Marcus had seemed to be taking too much notice, but then Kit didn't know him well enough to really say whether he had been or not. But other than telling her briefly earlier that he had been delayed getting ready for dinner by a telephone call from Andrea, he hadn't mentioned her again. The fact that he had left the room ten minutes ago, quickly followed by Andrea if Mike was to be believed, and hadn't returned yet, seemed to mean that he had been...

'For your information, Marcus isn't my boyfriend,' she snapped, giving Mike a withering look. 'And don't presume to project your own moral failings onto other people!'

He gave her an admiring glance. 'You've grown up in the last seven months, Kit.'

'Oh, please!' Her look of disdain intensified. 'Haven't I already made it obvious that you hold absolutely no charm for me? To the point where I actually walked out on a very well paid job just to avoid being anywhere near you?'

The handsome face grew dark with anger. 'You always did consider yourself superior—'

'I did not!' she cut in indignantly, more stung by the

remark than he could possibly imagine. 'I simply didn't—and still don't,' she continued heatedly, 'find you in the least attractive!'

He appeared unmoved by her outburst. 'Well, you're wasting your time as far as Marcus Maitland is concerned.'

'It's my time to waste!' she came back tartly, turning away from the array of desserts, having suddenly lost her appetite.

She already knew how stupid it was for her to be attracted to Marcus, didn't need this obnoxious man to tell her so!

Mike shook his head, a taunting smile curving his lips. 'You're way out of your depth, Kit.'

Her eyes flashed deeply grey. 'I would much rather have depth than be shallow!' Like you, her words obviously implied.

So much so that even the thick-skinned Mike Reynolds couldn't help but know exactly what she meant, his handsome face once again flushed with anger as he grated, 'As long as you don't mind being just another pretty face.'

Kit gave him a pitying look. 'You're just being pathetic now,' she dismissed contemptuously, knowing that in a woman his behaviour would have been classed as bitchy rather than pathetic!

'"The truth always hurts"',' he quoted nastily.

Kit wasn't about to give up. 'You wouldn't recognize the truth if it jumped up and bit you on the nose!'

To her surprise Mike laughed at this insulting remark.

But his next move surprised her even more as he

reached out to pull her against him to kiss her on the mouth. Hard.

She jerked away angrily, totally bewildered by his action. 'What on earth—?'

'You always were a lot of fun, Kit,' he told her cheekily, a maliciously triumphant gleam in his eyes now.

'Yes, that's Kit, all right.' Marcus spoke from just behind her. 'Fun and laughter all the way!'

Kit's face paled as she turned to look at Marcus, feeling slightly sick as she saw the contempt in those deep blue eyes of his as he looked back at her.

Deservedly so, she acknowledged heavily, knowing that Mike had done this on purpose, that he must have seen Marcus's return and had deliberately kissed her.

She pulled sharply away from Mike, uncaring that his fingers bruised her arms as she did so. 'You can't possibly believe I was enjoying that?' She turned to Marcus disbelievingly.

He looked at her searchingly for several long seconds before turning back to Mike, his expression grimmer than ever. 'I believe you owe Kit an apology,' he said tersely.

'Do I?' Mike came back aggressively.

'Is there a problem?' Desmond Hayes enquired as he approached them, having obviously already seen that there was and moved smoothly away from the group he had been conversing with.

'Nothing I can't handle,' Marcus assured him tightly. 'I suggest that in future—' he turned back to Mike Reynolds '—you save your less than obvious charms for someone who is more interested in them than Kit appears to be!'

'And if I don't?' the other man challenged.

'That's up to you, of course.' Marcus shrugged. 'But I should warn you that I have no intention of letting you upset Kit.'

Kit could have wept at the scene that was unfolding in front of her eyes, couldn't believe this was happening.

'I believe that at the moment both you gentlemen are upsetting Kit,' Desmond intervened, at the same time putting a protective hand on her shoulder. 'I suggest we leave the two of you to sort this out in private.'

'That's fine by me,' Marcus snapped, his icy gaze not leaving Mike's angrily flushed face.

'And me,' Mike concurred, looking at Marcus with intense dislike. 'If anything, you're even more arrogant than your girlfriend,' he told Marcus.

Kit gasped. 'I told you, I'm not—'

'Leave them to it, my dear,' Desmond advised, turning her away from the other two men and back into the throng of the party. 'Don't you know better than to try to come between two males fighting over territory?' he chided, reaching out to take a glass of champagne from a passing waiter and hand it to her. 'Drink some of that,' he encouraged. 'It will make you feel better.'

Kit didn't feel anything was going to succeed in doing that as she saw Marcus and Mike leave the house by the French doors. Doors that very firmly closed behind them!

'They'll be fine,' Desmond assured her laughingly. 'I believe Marcus was a champion boxer when he was at Cambridge. Unless, of course, it's Mike Reynolds you're worried about?' He raised amused brows as the idea suddenly occurred to him.

'Not in the least,' Kit told him firmly, sipping her champagne agitatedly. 'Tell me, does hitting another man actually ever solve anything?'

'Not usually, no,' Desmond confirmed. 'But it makes you feel a hell of a lot better!' he said with relish.

Kit laughed too. It was impossible not to, this man's expression was so full of boyish mischief. In fact, it was easy to see, when he was amusingly charming like this, exactly why Desmond had been married three times.

'All the things you've heard about me are true,' Desmond said, those shrewd blue eyes seeming to read her thoughts exactly. 'Except one of them,' he added softly, suddenly serious. 'I don't intend letting my third wife divorce me. She's the love of my life,' he told Kit quietly as she looked at him enquiringly.

It was too much on top of everything else that had happened to her this evening; Kit's eyes filled with sudden tears at the utter desolation she detected in the gentleness of his voice.

'It does happen, you know,' Desmond told her candidly. 'The so-called biggest of womanizers, when they find the right woman, will never look at another one.'

'I'm sorry.' She bowed her head, searching through her small evening bag for the tissue she had placed in there earlier. 'I know I'm being silly. It's just—'

'You're falling in love with Marcus,' he said knowingly.

Kit raised her head to look around them worriedly, concerned that someone might hear their conversation, reassured when she saw that no one was listening. She turned back to Desmond. 'Of course I'm not falling in love with Marcus—'

'Of course you aren't,' Desmond echoed her words teasingly. 'In the same way I'm not still in love with my wife.'

Kit gave a rueful smile. 'No, I really mean it—'

'So do I,' Desmond encouraged sympathetically. 'Ah, the victor returns,' he said with satisfaction after a glance over her shoulder. 'No doubt battle-scarred but victorious!'

Kit was almost afraid to turn round and see which one of the two men had just re-entered the house, Marcus or Mike. Not that she thought for a moment that it wouldn't be Marcus; there was just no comfort in it, knowing how furious he was with her.

She sighed, the tingling sensation she felt down her spine telling her that it was indeed Marcus who had just re-entered the house. And that he was making his way across the room to where they stood talking. 'I shall have to leave, of course—'

'You most certainly will not,' Desmond told her firmly, his hand once again clasping her shoulder. 'You're the only thing that's making this whole week-end bearable!'

'How touching,' drawled that all-too-familiar voice. 'Really, Kit,' Marcus said with hard derision as he moved to stand beside her, his shrewd gaze having taken in Desmond's proprietary hold on her, 'you're turning into quite the *femme fatale*!'

'She *is* a *femme fatale*,' Desmond told him happily. 'Beautiful. With a delightful sense of humour. Sensuous. Deliciously—calm down, Marcus,' he ordered as the younger man made an impatient movement. 'You can't go around fighting every man Kit so much as talks to, you know.'

Poor Desmond had this all so wrong, it would have been laughable if it weren't so tragic. She was falling in love with Marcus. But he certainly didn't feel the same way about her, despite his defence of her just now. And she very much doubted that he appreciated the suggestion that he did!

'Ah, to add to the intrigue, the lovely Andrea returns,' Desmond observed speculatively as Andrea Revel came back into the room.

The beautiful, sensuous, delicious Andrea Revel, Kit acknowledged heavily, knowing that the other woman really was everything that she wasn't herself. Andrea also looked stunningly attractive this evening in a bright red silk sheath of a dress that clung to her voluptuous curves. A fact she was obviously completely aware of as she strolled across the room to rejoin Derek Boyes.

Frankly, Kit had had enough of all of them for one evening!

'I'm afraid I have a headache.' She spoke to Desmond Hayes, deliberately keeping her gaze averted from the broodingly silent Marcus, one quick glance having shown her that, despite what Desmond had said, he showed no visible battle scars. But the fact that Mike Reynolds hadn't reappeared seemed to say that Desmond was right about which man had been the victor. 'If you will excuse me?' she added for politeness' sake only, not waiting for a response from either man before she turned and hurriedly left the room, looking to neither left nor right as she did so. She certainly didn't want to see Catherine Grainger again before she went to bed!

What a disaster of a weekend this was turning out

to be! There wasn't a single person here that she wanted to be with. Although Desmond Hayes had been something of a surprise these last few minutes, not at all what she had expected. Surprisingly, she actually found herself liking him. He—

'Oh, no, you don't!' Marcus grated gruffly, grasping the bedroom door as Kit would have closed it behind her.

Kit turned to look at him apprehensively. She had been completely unaware of him following her up the stairs—not surprising really, when her thoughts had been so full of the misery she had endured the last couple of hours!

'Let's go inside,' Marcus said, not waiting for her answer before moving past her into the bedroom.

Kit followed slowly, shutting the door quietly behind her, sensing his reproving gaze on her before she even looked at him. But once she had looked at him, she wished that she hadn't, the grimness of his voice more than reflected in his harshly set features!

'Well, you've certainly made a spectacle of yourself this evening, haven't you?' he said scornfully, thrusting his hands into his trouser pockets as he stared across the room at her.

'I have?' She gasped her indignation, feeling her anger starting to rise. 'I'm not the one who spent fifteen minutes out of the room with one woman and then came back and started acting all proprietorial about another one!' She glared at him accusingly, well past the mood of caution. And if Marcus sacked her for her outspokenness—fine! She really wasn't sure how they were going to continue to work together after this weekend, anyway.

'I'm flattered that you actually took note of the time,' he drawled.

'I didn't,' she told him swiftly. 'Mike was the one who noticed Andrea following you out of the room, and Desmond remarked on her return.' She threw her evening bag down on the bed. 'I couldn't give a damn what you do!' Her eyes sparkled deeply grey in her anger. 'Or, in fact, who you do it with!'

Marcus was very still, only a nerve pulsing in his jaw to tell of his own fury. 'Couldn't you?' he prompted softly.

'No!' she assured him decisively. 'As for going outside with Mike Reynolds—! Did the two of you actually have a fight?' She still found that whole scene unbelievable.

'Nothing so crude, Kit,' Marcus responded tersely. 'There are far subtler ways of dealing with a man like Mike Reynolds than resorting to physical violence. But how the hell do you even know a man like him? He said something about the two of you being involved seven months ago?' His eyes had narrowed to blue slits.

Kit gave a frustrated shake of her head. 'I thought you said you had read my résumé?'

'So I have,' Marcus confirmed with a perplexed frown. 'But what does that have to do with—?' He broke off abruptly, grimacing self-derisively as he momentarily closed his eyes.

'Exactly,' she bit out disgustedly, knowing the truth had finally dawned. 'Mike Reynolds is a prime example of what is meant by sexual harassment in the workplace. I utterly detest the man,' she finished with a shudder of distaste.

'Perhaps I should have hit him, after all,' Marcus muttered.

'Not on my account, no,' Kit assured him hastily.

He gave a ragged sigh. 'It seems I owe you an apology.'

'Accepted,' Kit said gruffly. 'Now would you please leave my bedroom?' She really had had quite enough for one day!

He drew in a harsh breath. 'One way or another, this has been—quite an enlightening evening, hasn't it?'

For whom? It certainly wasn't anything that Kit would want to live through again.

'Perhaps,' she returned noncommittally. 'But in the circumstances, I think it might be best if I were to leave here tomorrow.'

Before anything else disastrous happened!

'Because of Mike Reynolds?' Marcus queried. 'I believe he's leaving himself in the morning.'

Her eyes widened. 'Your doing?'

'My doing,' Marcus confirmed levelly.

Okay, so the Mike Reynolds problem might have been dealt with. But that still left Catherine Grainger...

'I would still rather leave,' Kit told him determinedly, knowing it was for the best.

Marcus paused for a moment. 'Because of my behaviour this evening?' He grimaced. 'First I accuse you of disloyalty, then I question your friendship with Mike Reynolds!'

'Partly because of that,' she answered cautiously.

He looked at her directly. 'But also because...?' he prompted.

Because a part of her had felt pleased at the way he had defended her against Mike Reynolds, and the fact that he hadn't seemed to like Desmond Hayes talking to her, either. But, ultimately, she had known it wasn't real, that it was only male pride on Marcus's part. To remain here for the rest of the weekend, posing as the woman in his life, would only give her false hopes.

She forced a smile. 'I just think it's for the best. Besides,' she went on, 'I'm sure Miss Revel will be only too pleased to keep you company.'

'And if it isn't Andrea that I want to keep me company?'

He was suddenly standing much too close for comfort, and Kit was easily able to feel the heat of his body, the warmth of his breath stirring the loose tendrils of hair at her temples.

She swallowed hard, at the same time forcing herself not to take a step backwards, determined not to let him see the effect his closeness was having on her. 'But we both know that it is,' she persisted.

'Do we?'

'Yes,' she said firmly, her eyes meeting his steadily. 'You said as much when we arrived here and you mentioned not making a scene.'

'What makes you think I was referring to Andrea…?'

Well, he certainly couldn't have been referring to her because of the friendly way Mike Reynolds had talked to her—could he…?

Marcus continued to look at her for several long seconds, finally taking a step backwards. 'How about we discuss this again in the morning?'

'How about we don't?' she came back heavily.

To her surprise, Marcus grinned, a completely humorous grin that warmed his eyes and curved his lips over even white teeth.

'It certainly is different being away on business with you rather than Lewis!'

Kit's own mouth quirked, relieved that the tension between them seemed to have broken. Although that didn't change her resolve to put as much distance tomorrow between herself and Desmond Hayes's house as was possible. As much distance between herself and Catherine Grainger as was possible...

'I would think it would be,' she conceded dryly.

Marcus chuckled now, his bad humour obviously dissipated. 'No borrowing his aftershave when I forget my own, for one thing,' he teased.

'Or socks and underwear,' Kit came back playfully.

'I draw the line at the underwear!' Marcus assured her dryly. 'The socks at a pinch, maybe, but—'

'Please go back downstairs and join the party!' Kit cut the conversation short.

Marcus sobered, looking at her intently now. 'You'll be okay up here on your own?'

'Of course,' she assured him easily.

A few more hours and she might be able to get away from here completely.

Away from the possibility of finding herself alone with Catherine Grainger again...!

CHAPTER EIGHT

THERE was someone in her bedroom!

Kit wasn't sure what had woken her: an unexpected noise, a sixth sense? But something had certainly disturbed her sleep and now she was aware of another person in the room with her—even though she couldn't see them in the dark shadows of the room, she could hear the soft sound of their breathing.

'Marcus?' she called tentatively.

She had no idea what he would be doing creeping about her bedroom during the early hours of the morning. But there again, he certainly hadn't seemed to have too much hesitation about walking into her bedroom unannounced yesterday evening!

The fact that she received no answer to her query convinced her that she was right in thinking it wasn't him...

'Who is it?' she said sharply, sitting up as she desperately tried to see into the shadows. 'Who's there?' she demanded as anger started to replace her apprehension.

If someone was trying to frighten her, then they were succeeding, and if they were trying to frighten her, then they deserved her anger!

'I said—' She broke off abruptly, her wrist grasped between tight fingers as she reached out to turn on the bedside light.

'I heard you, Kit,' came the unmistakable voice of Mike Reynolds.

'What are you doing in my bedroom?' Kit gasped disbelievingly, moving frantically across to one side of the bed as she felt him sit on the other side of it. 'How dare you—?'

'Be quiet, Kit,' he rasped, maintaining that steely grasp of her wrist. 'And don't be naïve; you know exactly why I'm here.'

'No, I—'

'Yes,' he cut in forcefully. 'To be honest, I couldn't quite believe my luck, when, instead of coming in here to join you when he came up to bed half an hour ago, I saw Maitland go into the room next door.'

Kit's eyes widened as she once again tried to see Mike's face in the darkness. 'You've been outside watching my bedroom?' Somehow just the thought of that made her skin crawl.

Mike gave a disgusted snort. 'What else did I have to do with my time after Maitland's threatening behaviour earlier?'

'Marcus didn't threaten you,' she defended, wishing now that Marcus had actually hit Mike—the verbal warning alone obviously hadn't worked!

'I thought your delicate sensibilities might prefer that description to the arrogant bastard he really is!' Mike said contemptuously.

'Isn't it a little late for you to be thinking of my delicate sensibilities?' she suggested, her vision having finally adjusted to the dim moonlight. She was able to see Mike's face now, if not his actual features. 'You have to leave, Mike,' she told him.

'And if I don't choose to?'

'Then I'll scream,' she informed him determinedly. 'Marcus is in the bedroom next door,' she added as a deterrent, knowing that Mike was a coward at heart.

He gave a humourless laugh. 'Poor little Kit,' he taunted. 'So naïve. So trusting. Your boyfriend is no longer in his room next door!' he informed her with hard satisfaction. 'Maitland only stayed a couple of minutes before leaving again. And he hasn't come back. Now, I don't know about you, but considering how thick he and Andrea Revel have been the last few months, I would say it's pretty easy to guess exactly whose bed he's in right now! Wouldn't you?'

Yes, she would, Kit accepted heavily, angry with Marcus for putting her in such an embarrassing position, but even more upset that he had left her an easy target for Mike Reynolds!

'Will you just leave?' she said stiffly. 'Before you do something we're both going to regret,' she added warningly.

'Oh, come on, Kit,' Mike cajoled. 'For goodness' sake, lighten up, will you? After all, we're old friends.' His tone was persuasive as his hand moved caressingly up her arm.

'Are you totally thick, or just plain stupid?' she challenged, annoyance easily overcoming her fear. 'I do not find you attractive. I have no intention of becoming involved with you. In fact, I'm sure I've made it perfectly plain that I don't even like you!' she finished frustratedly.

'Do you realise your boyfriend has persuaded Desmond to throw me out of here first thing in the morning?' The cajoling tone had turned to fury, and his hand tightened about her arm.

'Not soon enough, as far as I'm concerned!' Kit came back heatedly.

'Now just—'

'Or me!' rasped an authoritative voice that Kit easily knew belonged to Marcus. At the same time she felt Mike's hand release her arm as Marcus landed a punch on his jaw, which threw him off the bed.

'Get your things together now, Reynolds, and just leave!' Marcus was standing gloweringly over Mike as Kit at last managed to reach the switch for the bedside light. 'And I would advise you not to show your face anywhere near me in the next decade!'

Mike got slowly to his feet, the slight discolouration on his jaw already visible. And, despite her earlier protests about physical violence, Kit knew that she felt no regret at Marcus's action. In fact, she felt like hitting Mike herself!

'Playing musical beds, Maitland?' Mike sneered. 'One woman won't play, so you've come back to try the one in reserve?'

Marcus's eyes narrowed dangerously. 'I have no idea what you're talking about, Reynolds,' he rasped. 'Neither do I have any wish to know. Just go!'

'What do you think, Kit?' Mike turned to her tauntingly. 'Second-best about your limit, is it?' He gave a derisive smile as she wasn't quick enough to hide the flinch his hurtful words inflicted.

She knew he was being deliberately nasty, knew he was enjoying her discomfort, but there was so much truth behind his words that for the moment she couldn't think of anything to say.

'Go,' Marcus repeated in carefully controlled tones.

Mike went, slowly, nonchalantly, as cockily sure of himself as ever.

Kit's shoulders slumped once he had left the room, reaction starting to set in as she began to shake. Amazingly, she had no doubts in her mind that if Marcus hadn't come in when he had Mike really would have tried to force himself on her.

What made someone behave in that way? She had made it more than obvious that she disliked him, that she didn't find him attractive, that she certainly didn't want any sort of relationship with him, and yet he had still persisted. Maybe she had led a sheltered life, but she didn't understand that sort of behaviour...

'What on earth possessed you to let that man into your bedroom—?'

'I beg your pardon?' Kit rounded on Marcus disbelievingly, her eyes widely accusing as incredulity took over from the near-collapse she had felt coming on.

His mouth was a grimly set line. He was dressed only in the white silk shirt and trousers to his black dinner suit, having discarded the jacket. 'You knew what sort of man he was, so what on earth—?'

'Possessed me to invite him into my bedroom?' Kit finished through gritted teeth, getting out of bed, perfectly respectable in her coffee-coloured satin pyjamas, but reaching out to pull on the matching robe anyway. She hadn't thought that she would have her bedroom invaded in this way, not by one man, but two!

'Exactly,' Marcus agreed.

Kit gave an indignant sigh, at the same time tying the belt to her robe securely about the slenderness of her waist. 'It's all your fault,' she began.

'My fault?' he echoed as his head rose incredulously.

'And just how do you account for that, when I did everything in my power earlier this evening—apart from actually hitting the man!—to dissuade him from coming anywhere near you again?' His mouth twisted scathingly.

'He said you threatened him,' Kit accused.

'Obviously not strongly enough,' Marcus responded. 'I'm just surprised at you for inviting him into your room after that.'

'You just don't get it, do you?' she rejoined impatiently. 'I didn't invite Mike in here; he broke in while I was asleep. After first ascertaining that you had crept off to Andrea's bedroom, of course.'

'That I had—! What do you mean, he broke in?' Marcus seemed to think this part of her conversation was much more important than answering her other accusation.

Kit didn't agree with him, knew that if Marcus hadn't gone off to Andrea's bedroom Mike would never have dared to enter her bedroom in the way that he had.

She was also aware that this might be misdirected anger—but she had to blame someone, didn't she?

'Exactly what I said.' She moved away impatiently. 'The man needs locking up!'

Marcus remained silent for several nerve-racking moments and then he slowly nodded. 'We can do that,' he murmured harshly. 'If what you say is true—'

'Of course what I say is true!' Kit turned on him indignantly. 'I don't tell lies.'

'Look, Kit,' Marcus's expression softened slightly as he seemed to take in her agitated, wide-eyed appearance, 'I don't think losing your temper with me is going to solve anything—'

'Why isn't it?' she exclaimed. 'If it wasn't for you I wouldn't even be here. And if it wasn't for that, I wouldn't have been subjected to Mike Reynolds's unwanted advances! Neither would I have had to meet—' She broke off then, realising—almost too late!—exactly what she had been about to say.

The last thing she wanted to do was introduce the subject of Catherine Grainger to this already explosive situation!

'Yes?' Marcus prompted, dark brows raised enquiringly.

'Desmond Hayes,' she substituted defensively, only too aware of the seriousness of the slip she had almost made. 'Although, of the three of you, I think I prefer his company!'

Marcus's brows rose even higher. 'I noticed that the two of you seemed to be getting on well together, but—' He gave an incredulous shake of his head. 'Kit, you'll only end up getting hurt if you fall for Desmond,' he warned darkly.

'Oh, for goodness' sake!' She glared at him, two bright spots of angry colour in her cheeks. 'I said that, so far this weekend, his is the company I prefer, not that I'm attracted to him! Does everything have to come down to this male female attraction thing?'

His mouth twisted wryly. 'No, of course not. Although, it's usually a relevant factor.'

'Not to me,' she sighed. 'For your information, the only thing I've been able to learn this weekend by observing and listening, as you put it, is that Desmond is still very much in love with his wife!' She was breathing hard in her indignation, her chin raised challengingly, nipples roused beneath her robe.

A fact Marcus seemed very aware of as his gaze moved slowly over her.

Making Kit aware at the same time, the flush in her cheeks caused by something else entirely now, a wild fluttering in her chest, her breath seeming constricted in her throat, every inch of her tingling skin seeming as aware of Marcus as he was of her.

Not the most ideal situation to find oneself in at almost three o'clock in the morning when alone with a man you already knew yourself to be half in love with!

Although he had certainly done little to encourage those feelings this evening!

Kit straightened, her hands thrust defensively into the pockets of her robe. 'I think it's time you left, Marcus,' she told him, instantly wishing she had sounded more convincing.

'Yes,' he acknowledged with as little conviction.

She swallowed hard, her tongue moving nervously across her bottom lip, instantly knowing that had been the wrong thing to do as Marcus's gaze darkened, a nerve pulsing in his jaw.

After the noise and bustle of the evening, it was all so quiet about them, the house itself seeming asleep. Only the beat of Kit's heart, it appeared to her, sounded loudly in the silence.

Her eyes widened as Marcus slowly took two steps towards her. Her throat felt constricted so that she couldn't speak, not when he stood in front of her, not when he took her into his arms, not when his head lowered as his lips took gentle possession of hers.

His kiss deepened as passion exploded between

them. Marcus's tongue moved questioningly against her lower lip and Kit's response was to draw him deeper inside her.

He felt so right against her, their bodies moulded together as if two halves of a whole, Marcus's hands moving caressingly the length of her spine before tightening on her lower back to pull her into his hardness.

Warmth spread through her lower body at this evidence of his own arousal, her neck arching as Marcus's lips moved down its length to the sensitive hollows beneath.

Kit could only groan longingly as he pushed aside her robe and pyjama top to take one hardened nipple into the moist warmth of his mouth, sucking her deep inside him as his tongue lathed that sensitive tip.

Kit felt as if she were on fire, the centre of that fire situated at the very heart of her, her hands clinging to the broad width of his shoulders as his hand moved caressingly to her other breast, his thumb moving delicately, oh, so delicately, over the hardened tip.

She had never known such pleasure in her life, felt her control rapidly slipping away from her, her response to his caresses instinctive, as if her body had always known his touch, his caress.

A sob caught in her throat as she realised she was in love with this man, a part of her knowing this was just too much on top of everything else that had happened to her.

Marcus instantly pulled back slightly, raising his head to look at her with concerned blue eyes. 'I won't hurt you, Kit,' he promised.

It wasn't him she was afraid of—it was her own newly realised emotions!

Because she was already in love with Marcus. Deeply. Irrevocably. Knew it as surely as she knew her name.

And he was making love to her in such a way that she knew there could be only one way of this ending. Unless she put a stop to it—now!

Offence was her best form of defence... 'Marcus, haven't both of us had enough—excitement, for one evening?' she ventured.

'What do you mean?'

'Me, by having Mike invade my bedroom in the way that he did. And you, because—Andrea Revel,' she concluded, able to ease out of his arms now as his hands fell back to his sides, straightening her robe back into place as she moved even further away.

'Andrea?' Marcus repeated in a puzzled voice. 'What does she have to do with us?'

'Us?' Kit repeated, feeling more in control now that she had put some distance between them. Although she had no doubt that the memory of their closeness would haunt her dreams—day as well as night!—for a very long time. 'There is no ''us'', Marcus,' she responded quietly.

'Exactly what are you accusing me of where Andrea is concerned?' Marcus demanded, his expression stormy now.

'I'm not accusing you of anything,' she returned with more bravado than she really felt. If Marcus were to so much as touch her again, she knew she would be in his arms, with no thought of what tomorrow might bring! 'I told you, Mike only came in here earlier because he saw you go off to Andrea's bedroom.'

'He might have seen me leave my bedroom,' Marcus

conceded. 'But what makes either of you think it was in order to pay Andrea a nocturnal visit?'

Kit gave a shrug. 'It's obvious the two of you are still involved.'

'Says who?' he came back.

'Says anybody who looks at the two of you, apparently,' she returned, remembering all too easily how even the insensitive Mike Reynolds had taunted her about the relationship.

Marcus drew in a harsh breath. 'For your information, I went downstairs to enjoy a cigar with Desmond,' he explained. 'He was kind enough to invite me to join him. But for the record,' he continued coldly, 'as I've already told you, Andrea and I are finished. Totally. Irrevocably.' He walked purposefully to the adjoining bedroom door to wrench it open. 'I've told Desmond we shall be leaving tomorrow. He would prefer that we make it after lunch; is that going to be okay with you?'

'Fine,' Kit accepted numbly, just wishing he would go now and leave her alone to try and regain some of her shattered defences.

He paused in the open doorway. 'You know, Kit, I don't know what I've done to give you this—unflattering opinion you seem to have of me, but I can assure you that I do not make love to one woman while being involved with another!'

She swallowed hard, easily able to discern the scorn in his tone. But she was just too tired, too emotionally raw from her newly realised love for him, still too physically aware of him, to try to make any sense out of what had been a disturbing, confused evening.

'Goodnight, Kit,' Marcus said gruffly when it became obvious she had nothing else to say.

'Goodnight,' she echoed shakily, managing to remain standing upright until he had left the room.

When she collapsed shakily back onto the bed, at last allowing the tears that had been threatening for the last hour to overflow and cascade hotly down her cheeks.

Was this nightmare never going to end?

CHAPTER NINE

'I UNDERSTAND there was some sort of—situation, in your bedroom last night?'

Kit forced herself not to move on the sun lounger on which she lay beside the swimming pool, even though the sound of Catherine Grainger's voice had been enough to bring her eyes wide open behind the sunglasses she wore.

Unlike Kit, Catherine was fully dressed, albeit in a cool green linen sundress that showed her overall suntan to advantage. Kit, on the other hand, was wearing the black bikini she had bought for her holiday last year, her skin colour still creamy magnolia; she hadn't gone away on holiday yet this year.

Despite receiving no response to her question, Catherine Grainger made herself comfortable on the adjacent lounger, as beautifully composed as she had been yesterday; her hair was perfectly styled and her skin smooth, despite her being in her late sixties.

In fact, Kit knew *she* wouldn't mind being in this prime condition at the age of sixty-seven!

Which admission was enough to make her sit up a little straighter on her lounger, totally, she instantly realised, giving away her wakeful state.

'I thought you were awake.' Catherine Grainger nodded her satisfaction, her own sunglasses hiding silver eyes that Kit nevertheless knew to be totally shrewd and calculating.

'Did you?' Kit returned with cool uninterest.

'Oh, yes.' The older woman nodded again. 'It was the tapping of your fingers on the arm of your lounger that gave you away.'

Something Kit instantly stopped doing. Not that she was surprised to learn she had been doing something so mind-numbingly repetitive; after last night she was having trouble stringing two thoughts together, let alone making any sense of them!

It had been impossible for her to sleep after Marcus had left her room last night, because of a combination of anger towards Mike Reynolds and sheer frustration where Marcus was concerned—her body still remembered his kisses and caresses even if her mind was trying desperately to shut them out!

All in all, she'd not had a good night's sleep, and she had come outside early this morning to claim a lounger beside the pool, pushing the barrier of sunglasses onto the bridge of her nose in the hope of avoiding having to speak to any of the other people at this weekend party. Marcus, in particular!

Not, it appeared, that she need have worried about him too much; a maid cleaning beside the pool had informed her that Marcus had gone horse-riding with their host early this morning and wasn't expected to return until mid-morning.

A pity she hadn't been as fortunate where Catherine Grainger was concerned.

'So...' Catherine removed her own sunglasses to turn those penetrating silver-grey eyes on Kit '...why is it, when you assure me that we have never met before, I have the distinct impression we know each other?'

Every defensive bone in Kit's body cried out to tell this woman the truth, to tell Catherine Grainger exactly why she had this feeling of familiarity, of who and what it was that gave her that feeling!

But another part of her knew she couldn't do that; she had no intention of betraying a confidence given to her, and to do so would hurt other people as well as herself.

Kit turned her head to look at Catherine. 'I can assure you—once again!—that the two of us have never met before,' she said with complete honesty.

What would Marcus think, what would he say or do, if he could see Catherine Grainger talking to Kit now? It would no doubt arouse his suspicions all over again about where those leaks from his office were coming from—when, in point of fact, Kit wouldn't tell this woman the time of day!

'So you've said,' Catherine acknowledged distantly, but still looking intensely at Kit with those piercing silver-grey eyes. 'So what did happen last night?'

Kit gave a start. Although why she was surprised was beyond her; Catherine Grainger was a woman who always got what she wanted, and that included answers to the questions she asked.

Except, not this time… 'I have no idea what you're referring to,' Kit dismissed.

And, in point of fact, she didn't, not specifically. Was Catherine referring to Mike Reynolds's unexpected visit to her bedroom, or Marcus's appearance following that? Whichever it was, it was none of Catherine's business!

'Oh, come on, Kit.' Catherine gave a hard laugh. 'A man pays an unwelcome visit to your bedroom in the middle of the night and you have no idea what I'm referring to? My dear, if that really is the case, then what an exciting life you must lead!'

Catherine's reference to an unwelcome visitor to her bedroom didn't help to enlighten Kit in the least; she could still just as easily be referring to Marcus's visit as Mike Reynolds's!

'Not particularly.' She answered the other woman tersely. 'As you say, it was unwelcome and, as such, I think it better to forget it ever happened.' In both cases. As far as Mike Reynolds was concerned, she hoped she never saw him again. With regard to Marcus's visit, she had to forget it if she intended to continue working for him.

'Just pretend it never happened, you mean?' the older woman mused. 'My dear, you certainly have spirit!'

And Kit had to stop herself from visibly gnashing her teeth at having Catherine Grainger, of all people, refer to her as 'my dear', not once, but twice. She wasn't Catherine Grainger's 'dear' anything, and never would be!

'Thank you,' she accepted briskly.

'I'm not sure that Desmond intends treating the situation as lightly as you seem able to,' Catherine announced.

Kit gave her a sharp look. 'What do you mean?'

Catherine shrugged. 'It happened in his home, my dear; not exactly pleasant. Especially if you decide to press charges later on.'

She had to be referring to Mike Reynolds's unwanted visit to Kit's bedroom, couldn't possibly think

Kit would press charges against *Marcus* for what had, after all, been a mutual passion.

'I won't,' Kit denied. 'The Mike Reynoldses of this world are, as you say, unpleasant, but hardly worth disrupting one's life for.'

'That's very commendable,' Catherine replied graciously. 'By the way, that's a really nasty bruise you have on your arm.'

Kit felt the colour flush her cheeks; she had put foundation cream on the discolouration caused by Mike clasping hold of her arm so tightly the night before, but unfortunately she hadn't quite managed to hide the colours-of-the-rainbow effect in the shape of fingers!

Kit found herself disliking this woman more than ever for drawing attention to her bruising. Was it any wonder that—?

'My fault, I'm afraid,' Marcus remarked easily as he dropped down onto Kit's lounger, bending forward to kiss her bruised arm. 'A little over-enthusiasm on my part. Sorry, darling,' he told her throatily.

Kit, having dreaded seeing Marcus again after what had happened between them last night, suddenly found herself very pleased to see him. Especially as he seemed to have summed the situation up at a glance—well…some of it!—and come to her rescue.

She had been so caught up in her conversation with Catherine Grainger that she hadn't even noticed his approach. But now she could only admire how handsome he looked in his riding jodhpurs and a loose white shirt.

'Marcus,' she greeted warmly, her relieved smile telling him how grateful she was for his interruption.

'Well, it seems I must leave you two lovebirds alone,' Catherine Grainger murmured as she stood up.

'A word of advice, though, Marcus...' She paused beside them. 'Kit's skin is far too delicate and fair for such rough lovemaking!' She strolled away towards the house.

'Why, that interfering old—'

'Now, now, Kit, let's not be bitchy,' Marcus interrupted her with amusement, his blue eyes reflecting his smile. 'Catherine is such a cold person herself she's probably forgotten what lovemaking is like, rough or otherwise!'

Kit grinned. 'Now who's being bitchy?'

He straightened to look at her critically. 'Did Reynolds really do that to you last night?' His mouth had thinned as he inspected the marks on her arm.

'Yes—but it doesn't matter,' she quickly dismissed as Marcus's expression darkened even more. She reached out to pick up her towelling robe and pull it on, hoping that hiding the bruises might take Marcus's mind off their existence. She should have known better. Marcus was nothing if not single-minded.

'Oh, yes, it matters,' he assured her softly.

'Please leave it, Marcus.' She put a pleading hand on his arm. 'He's gone now.' Mike's departure was the first thing she had checked on when she had come downstairs this morning. 'It's enough that as many people know about it as they do.'

Marcus looked at her searchingly. 'I owe you an apology for last night—'

'Couldn't we just forget about that too?' she said self-consciously.

'Can you forget about it?' he replied huskily.

Forget Marcus kissing her? Forget Marcus caressing

her? Forget the way he had aroused her? Forget the way he had been aroused by her?

No—of course she couldn't forget about it. But the alternative, of leaving his employment and never seeing him again, wasn't acceptable, either.

She couldn't quite meet his searching gaze now. 'I can try,' she told him slowly.

Marcus gave a shake of his head. 'I don't know what the hell came over me, talking to you in the way that I did! And as for—'

'Please!' Inwardly Kit cringed; the last thing she wanted was to hear his regrets about kissing and caressing her.

'Perhaps you're right,' he allowed heavily, standing up too. 'Incidentally, what were you and Catherine Grainger talking about before I arrived? Besides Reynolds, of course.'

Kit gave him a darting look, unable to read anything from his bland expression. Deliberately so? She wasn't sure. But it was obvious from Marcus's question that he was still uneasy about her conversations with his arch business rival, that maybe he did still suspect her in some way.

She actually had no idea why Catherine Grainger kept singling her out in this way.

She only knew the reason she would rather the other woman didn't do so!

She gave Marcus a narrow-eyed look. 'You still don't trust me, do you…?'

'Kit, I have no idea who to trust any more,' he answered truthfully. 'I only know that when I do find the traitor in my camp, they are going to wish they had never been born!'

She swallowed hard, not doubting for a moment that he meant what he said. Should she tell him now of her past connection to Catherine Grainger, of the reason she disliked the woman so much she couldn't possibly be the one who was passing her information?

She shuddered just at the thought of doing that, at the contempt she would see in his face if he knew the truth. Besides, it wasn't her secret to tell...

She gave an abrupt shake of her head. 'Then it's just as well it isn't me, isn't it?'

'Isn't it?' he returned hardly.

Their gazes locked in mutual challenge, Kit determined not to be the one to back down.

Marcus finally gave in. 'I think I'll just go upstairs and take a shower. I've finished talking to Desmond, so we can leave before lunch if you would—'

'Oh, yes!' she accepted quickly. 'I can't wait to get away from here,' she admitted abruptly.

'Believe me, it isn't the most successful twenty-four hours I've ever known, either. Oh, and by the way, you were right about Desmond.' He paused.

Kit gave him a curious look. 'About his still being in love with his wife, you mean?'

'That—' Marcus nodded '—and the fact that the rumours concerning his financial problems did originate from him.'

'They did?' She had merely been guessing when she had made that comment yesterday, hadn't really thought there would be any truth in it.

'Yes,' Marcus went on. 'Although not for the reason we supposed. He's actually in no financial difficulty at all, but he thought that if his wife believed he was she might come back to him.'

Kit's expression was perplexed. 'Isn't it usually the other way around...?'

'That's very cynical of you, Kit,' he teased. 'Obviously you've never met the latest Mrs Hayes.'

'Well, of course I haven't met her! I don't usually mix in such exalted company as I have this weekend,' she shot back.

'The exalted bit is certainly a matter of opinion!' Marcus responded wryly. 'I can think of several people here this weekend who certainly don't come under that heading!'

Mike Reynolds and Catherine Grainger being two of them, Kit easily guessed.

'So can I,' she agreed dully.

'I'm sure you can,' he allowed flatly. 'Anyway, the bottom line is that Jackie wants children and Desmond is terrified at the thought. But as he also loves his wife to distraction...'

'He came up with the idea of starting a rumour that he's in financial difficulties in the hopes of winning Jackie back,' Kit realised.

'Yes,' Marcus confirmed.

'But didn't they discuss having children before they got married?'

'I have no idea,' Marcus told her lightly. 'Having only just started my career as a marriage guidance counsellor, I didn't think to ask that question!'

'And you're so highly qualified too!' She instantly felt the colour warm her cheeks at her unthinking outspokenness. 'What I meant to say was—'

'I know what you meant to say, Kit,' he assured her. 'As for Desmond, I felt quite sorry for him, actually.'

'Who did you feel sorry for, darling?' Andrea Revel

cut smoothly in on their conversation, moving to stand next to Marcus as she linked her arm loosely with his to look up at him.

Instantly making five-feet-ten-inches-tall Kit feel like a giraffe—and with about as much grace of movement!

The other woman looked gorgeous, of course, the skimpy green bikini she wore moulding to the perfection of her voluptuous curves, the tiny pieces of material leaving little to the imagination.

Not that Marcus needed imagination where this woman's curves were concerned, Kit reminded herself crossly.

Or that it was any of her business, she rebuked herself.

'Surely not Mike Reynolds?' Andrea persisted when she received no answer, green eyes glittering maliciously as she looked across at Kit.

'No, not Reynolds,' Marcus rasped, obviously having no intention of breaking Desmond's confidence by enlightening Andrea as to exactly whom he had been talking about.

Andrea arched blonde brows. 'I believe you had a little trouble with the man last night, Kit…?'

Did everyone here know what had happened in her bedroom last night? Although she didn't need to look far to know who had been Andrea Revel's informant!

She gave Marcus a glare before answering Andrea. 'Nothing that couldn't be sorted out,' she said tightly.

'Lucky for you that Marcus came back when he did,' Andrea drawled pointedly.

'Very,' Kit acknowledged tautly, knowing from the taunting glint in the other woman's catlike eyes that she was enjoying her discomfort thoroughly. 'If you'll both excuse me, I would like to go inside and dress?' she said stiltedly. 'You said we're leaving shortly, Marcus?'

'In about an hour,' he confirmed.

It couldn't be soon enough for her, Kit knew as she turned away from the sight of Andrea Revel leaning her curves into Marcus's body as the two of them whispered together.

Her heart ached as she acknowledged that Marcus wasn't exactly pushing Andrea away. Oh, she believed him when he said his relationship with Andrea was over before the two of them had come away together for the weekend, but that didn't mean that it couldn't be rekindled, did it? She didn't doubt that if Andrea Revel had any say in it then it certainly would be!

Just as she didn't doubt her own love for Marcus. Or that that love was of the everlasting variety.

What an idiot she was.

She had spent the last six months hiding her own attractiveness from Marcus, only to fall in love with him and wish that he would feel the same way about her.

What a futile hope…!

CHAPTER TEN

'YOU'RE very quiet?'

'I was under the impression you preferred it that way when you're driving.' Kit didn't even glance in Marcus's direction as he sat behind the wheel of his Jaguar, remaining relaxed back in her seat, her sunglasses once again perched protectively on the bridge of her nose.

'*Touché,*' he allowed. 'What are you going to do with the rest of your weekend?'

'What do you mean?'

'Well, you must have cancelled all your original plans in order to come away with me this weekend, and now we're returning early. And I won't expect you to come in to the office until Tuesday—after all, you've given up most of your Saturday.'

'Yes?' she acknowledged guardedly.

'I just wondered what you were going to do with all this sudden free time?'

She gave a puzzled smile. 'Whatever I usually do with my weekend, I suppose.'

'Which is?' he persisted.

'Marcus—er—Mr Maitland,' she corrected hastily.

'Marcus will do,' he told her dryly. 'After all, we're still out of the office,' he qualified.

'Okay,' she agreed slowly. 'But where is all this questioning leading?'

'It isn't leading anywhere.' He grimaced. 'At least—

I wondered if perhaps you would like to have dinner with me this evening?'

Kit became very still, slowly turning her head to look at him, glad that the surprise that must be in her eyes was hidden by her sunglasses. Was Marcus inviting her out on a date? But he couldn't be. Could he…?

'Why?' she finally said bluntly.

'Well, it's logical that you have to eat, and I have to eat, so I thought perhaps we might eat together,' he supplied.

Kit opened her mouth to answer him in the negative, and then closed it again. Logic, as far as she was concerned, had absolutely no place in any suggestion that the two of them have dinner together this evening!

But even so, she was tempted. What would it be like to actually go out for the evening with Marcus? To take her time getting ready for the evening, to be collected by Marcus and swept off to an exclusive restaurant for a meal, possibly even a club later.

She had no doubts that he would prove an interesting and charming companion. Or that she would absolutely love to spend the evening with him. What didn't make any sense was why he was asking her in the first place!

Unless it was just as he had said: he had to eat, she had to eat—and why not eat together?

'If it takes you this long to decide, maybe you should just forget I asked!'

'Maybe we should,' Kit agreed stiffly. 'I was thinking of going to see my parents,' she added lightly as she realised how rude she must have sounded.

'Really?' He gave her an interested look. 'Do they live in London?'

'No. Cornwall,' she replied awkwardly as she realised she was being rude again. 'I thought I would go down by train later this afternoon.'

'That's quite a way.' Marcus nodded. 'I could drive you there, if you would like?'

'Why on earth would you want to—? No,' she amended hastily, not even wanting to give him that particular opening. He was far too curious about her private life already, without trying to wheedle his way into meeting her parents; she could hardly accept such an offer from him without inviting him to stay the weekend too. Something she had absolutely no intention of doing! 'It's much quicker by train,' she dismissed, deliberately turning away to look out of the side window.

'So, no dinner this evening? Either in London or Cornwall,' he persisted.

'I'm afraid not,' she answered with a breeziness she didn't feel.

'What do your parents do in Cornwall?'

She gave him a sharp look. 'Do...?'

'As in work.'

'Oh.' She nodded. 'My mother looks after the house—cottage, really,' she amended. 'And my father paints.' She wished she had never mentioned her parents. And she wouldn't have done if it hadn't seemed like the ideal way of getting out of his dinner invitation without being rude.

'As in walls or canvases?'

'Marcus, I really don't think this is a line of questioning we should be pursuing.' She straightened uncomfortably in her seat.

'Line of questioning? Pursuing?' Marcus was incredulous. 'You sound like a lawyer defending her client. I was only showing an interest, Kit.'

'I know you were.' She sighed, her cheeks blushing warmly. 'I just—canvases. My father paints canvases,' she explained reluctantly.

'Really?' Marcus raised dark brows. 'Do I know him? Is he famous?'

'Would you expect him to be living in a cottage in Cornwall if he was!' Kit responded, knowing that she wasn't being strictly honest. There was plenty of money now for her parents to move to a larger, more comfortable home; they just preferred to stay at the cottage where they had lived since they had first married. 'I believe my father is what is usually known as a starving artist.'

'But not in a garret?' Marcus returned lightly.

'No.' She laughed, relaxing slightly. 'But the cottage is certainly—rustic.' She remembered that, until a few years ago, the cottage hadn't even had running water, her mother having to get water from a well in the garden until they had had the main water supply connected.

'Sounds wonderful.' Marcus smiled.

'It sounds it,' Kit conceded. 'And actually it is. If you don't mind roughing it a bit.' She had enjoyed a completely carefree childhood amongst the rugged hills of Cornwall, roaming for miles; it was what had given her her love of walking.

'I'm ashamed to say I've never tried,' Marcus admitted.

Was he still trying to persuade her into allowing him to drive her to Cornwall?

What would her parents make of him? Her father,

she knew, would find him the complete antithesis of himself, but somehow she still had a feeling that he would like the younger man. As for her mother—she would just be pleased to see Kit with a man, her hints of wishing to be a grandmother having increased during the last year or so.

Which was a very good reason for not giving into Marcus's persuasive tone.

The last thing she needed was her parents thinking she was actually involved with Marcus!

'I'm sorry.' She shook her head firmly. 'The cottage is simply too small to accommodate all four of us.'

'We could share,' he suggested.

'I said my father is an artist—not that he's an advocate of— Well, the fact that he married my mother within weeks of meeting her should tell you something about him,' she amended awkwardly; her parents were far from being prudes, would probably accept the idea if she brought a man home for the weekend. It was Kit who had a problem with it!

Marcus gave an appreciative nod. 'It tells me he's an astute man. They have obviously been married for some time, so I presume it's a happy marriage?'

'Very,' Kit confirmed unhesitantly.

'Then that's all that really matters, isn't it?'

She gave him a searching look. 'Is it?' Somehow it had never actually occurred to her, in light of his own brief relationships with women, that Marcus believed in love and marriage...

'Of course. Look at Desmond,' he reminded her. 'He made two serious errors in his first marriages, and now he's in love with and married to a woman thirty years his junior. He's making a bit of a mess of it at the moment, I grant you, but I have complete confidence in him seeing, before it's too late, what an idiot he's being.'

'Did you tell him as much?' Kit chuckled.

'Of course,' he confirmed unrepentantly. 'He *is* being an idiot. Second to actually finding the woman you love, having a child with that woman has to be the most wonderful experience of any man's life. Wouldn't you say?'

She would, yes. But she wouldn't have thought that Marcus would say so, too…

He gave her a glance, noting her thoughtful expression. 'You just didn't think I would say so, too, did you?' he guessed shrewdly.

Kit glared at him. 'Well, you hardly give the impression that marriage and a family are high on your list of priorities!'

'You have to meet the right woman to even begin to think in that vein.'

And he expected to find that 'right woman' by going out with women like Andrea Revel? Somehow Kit didn't think so.

But if Marcus did, who was she, a complete outsider, to say otherwise? Even if she did love him to distraction!

'I suppose so,' she conceded noncommittally. 'I had rather a disturbed night's sleep, would you mind if I had a little nap now?'

'Just as the conversation was getting interesting…' he murmured speculatively.

'Maybe to you,' she shot back, settling down comfortably in her seat. 'It's a matter of complete indifference to me.'

'Of course it is.'

Kit turned sharply at what she felt was a completely patronizing tone. 'Not every woman wants to get married and have children, you know,' she snapped.

'You do,' he insisted softly.

She gave him a frustrated glare. 'Maybe,' she finally accepted tersely. 'But if Mike Reynolds is an example of what men are like, then I would rather not bother, thank you!'

'He isn't,' Marcus assured her. 'At least, I hope he isn't!' he added frowningly. 'You don't think I'm like Mike Reynolds, do you?'

This conversation had taken an extremely strange turn as far as Kit was concerned—one she would rather not pursue!

'I've never thought about it,' she responded airily.

'I bet you haven't,' he returned, obviously not at all happy with the conversation himself now.

Kit closed her eyes, a little smile playing about her lips, as her last vision of Marcus was a most disgruntled expression as he struggled with the concept of there being any sort of comparison between himself and a man he obviously despised.

Not that there was, of course. But it wouldn't hurt to leave Marcus with that thought, anyway. It was certainly better than discussing her personal life!

As it was she had told him a lot more about herself, and her parents, than she had really intended doing. But, with any luck, that was the end of the subject...

'Sure I can't persuade you into letting me drive you to Cornwall?' Marcus pressed once he had parked his car outside her apartment building.

'Positive.' She pushed open the car door and got out.

'If I get a move on I'll be able to make the afternoon train,' she told him as he got out of the car too in order to take her bag out of the boot.

'This is goodbye, then.' Marcus stood beside her on the pavement.

Kit gave an incredulous laugh. 'Hardly, when I'll be seeing you in the office on Tuesday morning!'

'Not the same,' he said. 'I very much doubt you'll be strolling around the office in a bikini!'

'Very funny!' she replied, not at all happy with the way her cheeks flushed fiery red at his teasing.

'I wasn't trying to be funny, Kit,' he said quietly, dark blue gaze staring intently into hers.

'Well, you succeeded, anyway,' she told him, wishing she could break the intensity of that gaze, but knowing she couldn't, that it was simply beyond her at this moment.

How she loved this man! How she would love to accept his invitation to dinner, to drive her to Cornwall; anything to spend more time with him.

But ultimately she would only end up hurting herself more than she already had; despite the attraction that had flared up between them briefly this weekend, she knew she simply wasn't Marcus's type, and never would be.

'Kit, you have the most amazingly beautiful eyes I have ever seen,' he murmured gruffly, his gaze even more intense. 'Dark and soft, like grey velvet.'

Kit moistened her lips nervously, wishing—

'Don't do that!' he ground out suddenly, his gaze focused on her mouth now. 'Do you have any idea how provocative that is?' he groaned before his head bent and his mouth took fierce possession of hers.

She hadn't, no. But she did now!

Once again she melted as soon as Marcus's lips touched hers, both his hands cradling the sides of her face as he kissed her with searching passion, sipping and tasting, plundering, possessing.

Kit was aware only of Marcus as she clung to him, of the thrust of desire coursing through them both as her fingers tightly gripped the warm strength of his shoulders, of—

'Wow!' came an amused voice. 'Is that really you, Kit?'

Kit pulled sharply away from Marcus as she easily recognized that voice, turning to look at Penny as her flatmate came down the steps of their apartment building, dressed for her usual Saturday afternoon game of tennis with her fiancé, Roger.

'Penny!' Kit greeted lightly, almost afraid to look at Marcus after the desire that had blazed between them so suddenly.

And completely. How was she going to be able to work with Marcus day after day after this, when all she really wanted was to lose herself in his arms, to forget everything else but the fierce attraction they seemed to share?

'Penny...?' Marcus looked at Kit enquiringly.

'My flatmate,' Kit revealed with a certain amount of reluctance, knowing by the slight smile of satisfaction that suddenly curved his lips that Marcus really had nurtured the idea that her flatmate might be male! 'Penny Lyon. Marcus Maitland,' she introduced stiffly, knowing that Penny needed no explanation as to who and what Marcus was.

Although her friend could just be wondering what

Kit was doing kissing her boss out in the middle of the street! Could just be wondering? Penny would no doubt demand the full story as soon as she had Kit on her own again!

The problem with that was that Kit had no idea what the full story was where she and Marcus were concerned. Marcus seemed to be acquiring the habit of just taking her in his arms and kissing her whenever he felt like it. And it would be useless to deny that she responded to those kisses. But was there any more to it than that? As far as Kit was concerned, there was, but she had no idea what Marcus's motivation was.

Except that he seemed to like kissing her...

'I had a feeling that's who you were,' Penny told Marcus as the two of them shook hands. 'You're back early.' She looked enquiringly at Kit. 'I was expecting you to be away the whole weekend...?'

'Change of plan, I'm afraid,' Marcus was the one to answer Penny smoothly. 'We aren't delaying you from an appointment, are we?' he prompted with a pointed look at the tee shirt and the long display of bare leg beneath the shorts Penny was wearing in preparation for her game of tennis.

'Not in the least—but I can take a hint!' Penny replied laughingly.

'My dear, Miss Lyon—Penny?—I can assure you that if I wanted to be alone with Kit then I would just say so,' Marcus said.

'I had a feeling you might,' Penny acknowledged wryly. 'I'll see you later, Kit?'

She gave a thankful shake of her head; she needed to get her own thoughts about this weekend into some sort of order before subjecting herself to Penny's obvious interest in finding her kissing Marcus! 'I'm going to see my parents this afternoon,' she explained economically. 'I'll be back late tomorrow.'

'I'll look forward to it,' Penny assured her. 'Nice to meet you, Mr Maitland,' she added warmly.

'Marcus,' he insisted. 'Nice to meet you too, Penny.'

A smile remained on his lips only long enough for Penny to get into her car and drive away with a friendly wave of her hand.

At which time he looked down at Kit with accusing eyes. 'Yesterday you deliberately let me think your flat-mate was a man.'

'I did not,' Kit defended. 'I simply didn't say one way or the other.'

'Exactly,' he sighed impatiently. 'But you knew I had assumed it was a man.'

'I knew no such thing!' she denied calmly. 'If you chose to think that, then—'

'Kit, why are we arguing again?' He winced. 'The last thing I want to do at this moment is argue with you!'

One look at his face, at the glitter of intent in his blue gaze as it fixed on the pouting softness of her mouth, was enough to tell her what he did want to do with her!

But they simply couldn't continue to behave in this way, not if they were to continue working together. A break away from each other, to get things back into perspective, was exactly what they needed.

'I really do have to go, Marcus,' she told him after a glance at her wrist-watch. 'My train leaves in just under an hour,' she added pointedly.

He drew in a sharply disapproving breath at her haste. 'I had better let you go, then, hadn't I?'

That urge to ask him to come to Cornwall with her after all returned with a vengeance, the words actually on the tip of her tongue. A tongue she bit with sharp purpose, deliberately saying nothing.

'Fine,' Marcus said abruptly. 'Thank you for your help this weekend, Kit. I appreciate it.'

She gave a rueful smile. 'I don't think, with the situation that developed with Mike Reynolds, that I was much of an asset!' More of a liability, really!

He shook his head. 'Forget Mike Reynolds,' he dismissed. 'Desmond was the main reason for going this weekend, and he liked you very much.'

Her eyes widened. 'He did?'

'Oh, yes,' Marcus confirmed. 'I believe you had a word with him yourself before we left...?'

Actually, she had had several words with their host before leaving earlier, having decided she would probably never see Desmond Hayes again, so she might as well tell him exactly what she thought about his separation from his wife, and the reason for it. But she hadn't realised he had mentioned that conversation to Marcus...

She gave a self-conscious grimace. 'Did he say that I had?'

'He did.' Marcus nodded approvingly. 'On your advice, he's going to call Jackie this afternoon and hopefully meet up with her to discuss having half a dozen kids or so!'

'Half a dozen—!' Kit gasped. 'I don't think I said anything about six children...!'

Marcus grinned. 'Whatever you said, it was the right

thing. I have a feeling that Desmond and I are going to have quite a healthy business relationship in future.'

Then Kit had fulfilled her role as his personal assistant. Because that was all she was to him, no matter how much she might wish it were otherwise.

'What did you say to him to make him act so quickly?' Marcus looked at her searchingly.

'I think it was something along the lines of life being too short, and love being too hard to find to let it go because sometimes the commitment of that love might frighten us.'

Marcus's gaze became guarded. 'You sound like someone who has had experience of the emotion…?'

Only as regards her own parents. If her mother hadn't been so determined to be with the man she loved, if her father hadn't been that man, then Kit knew she would never have been born.

'Maybe,' she answered noncommittally.

Marcus stepped back from her. 'I'll let you get off, then.'

'Yes,' she agreed, knowing that one of them had to make a move. But also realising that neither of them seemed to want to do that. 'I have to catch my train,' she reminded Marcus firmly, giving him a quick smile before turning to run lightly up the stairs to open the door to her apartment building, determined not to look back, knowing it could be her undoing if she did.

All the time feeling as if she were leaving the biggest part of her standing outside on the pavement…

CHAPTER ELEVEN

'GOOD weekend?'

Kit looked up at the sound of Lewis Grant's voice. 'Not particularly,' she answered honestly.

'Oh?' He leant against the side of her desk, obviously in no hurry to go to his own office down the corridor.

She put aside the papers she had been working on for the last half an hour to give him her full attention. 'Those sort of house parties aren't really my scene.'

Lewis grinned understandingly. 'Lots of glitz and glamour on the surface—and knives being wielded behind the backs!'

'Something like that,' she said noncommittally.

To be perfectly honest, she really wasn't quite with it this bright and sunny Tuesday morning, was wishing herself anywhere but here.

Luckily, Marcus hadn't arrived in the office yet. Kit usually arrived half an hour or so before he did so that she could deal with any urgent correspondence and put it on his desk.

Lewis chuckled. 'I quite enjoy them, actually. But I can understand why some people wouldn't,' he sympathized.

Especially someone like her, Kit silently added. Prim Miss McGuire, the PA from No-Nonsenseville, was back in place this morning; after the intimacy that seemed to have developed between herself and Marcus over the weekend, she had thought it for the best. Not that she for a moment thought she would have Marcus chasing her around the desk at every opportunity; no, prim Miss McGuire was for her own protection—from her feelings towards Marcus!

'It was okay.' Kit returned her attention to Lewis.

'Any success with Desmond Hayes?' he enquired with interest.

'Not particularly,' she returned. 'I'm really not being a lot of help this morning, am I?'

'Probably tired after the weekend.' Lewis smiled understandingly.

'I still don't understand why Marcus didn't take me with him,' he mused. 'But there you are. I suppose—'

'Don't you have any work to do, Lewis?' Marcus barked as he came into Kit's office, dressed in one of the dark business suits and snowy white shirts he usually wore to work, briefcase in hand. 'Kit,' he added in tight acknowledgement.

'M—Mr Maitland,' she hastily corrected her initial slip of going to call him by his first name.

'Come through to my office, will you?' he instructed her curtly, his gaze cold as he looked at Lewis. 'Anything I can do for you?' he grated.

'Nothing at all,' the younger man said easily, not seeming too concerned by Marcus's mood.

'Then don't let us keep you,' Marcus responded, looking straight at Kit as he held his office door open.

Kit got up slowly to move across the room and enter Marcus's office, very aware of his brooding presence as he closed the door behind them with a firm click.

She turned to look at him. 'Don't you think you were a little rude to Lewis just now?'

'Was I?' he replied unconcernedly. 'I'm sure he'll get over it.' He placed his briefcase down beside his desk before sitting down in the high-backed leather chair behind it, resting his elbows on the desk as he looked at her over the top of the pyramid of his fingers. 'Why the hell are you dressed like that again?' he suddenly exclaimed.

Kit felt herself pale as she stared at him through her heavy, dark-rimmed glasses, her breath catching in her throat, in no doubt as to Marcus's annoyance; his face was grim, a nerve pulsing in his jaw.

'I thought it best,' she offered, moistening her lips with the tip of her tongue.

'And I thought I warned you about doing that,' Marcus snapped, his gaze focused on her mouth now.

Kit instantly clamped her lips together, the colour flooding back into her cheeks as she remembered what had happened the last time she had moistened her lips in that way in front of Marcus.

'Well?' he prompted harshly.

She flinched at his attack. 'Well, what…?'

He rose quickly to his feet, as if his mood was too big to be contained in a sitting position. 'Exactly what sort of man do you think I am? Don't answer that. The fact that you're back to wearing that ridiculous disguise tells me exactly what you think of me!'

What she thought of him? It was herself, the love she felt towards him, that she was trying to protect!

'I don't see how,' she said wearily.

'No?' He moved out from behind his desk to pace the room restlessly. 'I think I should warn you that I don't care for being put in the same category as your last boss!'

'Mike Reynolds…?' Kit repeated dazedly. 'But I—' She broke off, frowning across at Marcus now. 'I never for a moment thought that you were in the least like him…' But she could hardly explain that it was herself she was trying to protect by once again becoming Prim Miss McGuire from No-Nonsenseville!

'Oh, give me a break, Kit,' Marcus came back. 'You've already told me exactly why you started wearing those ridiculous glasses and unflattering clothes. The fact that you're back to wearing them today implies you still think you need some sort of protection from my obviously unwanted advances!'

What would he say if she were to tell him that what she really wanted to do—not just now, but all the time!—was throw herself into his arms and have him make love to her? Here. Now.

'And just when did you intend telling me about your father?' Marcus continued.

Kit blinked at this sudden change of subject. 'My father…?'

Marcus nodded tersely. 'Your father is Tom McGuire!' he accused.

'I know who he is,' she answered levelly.

'So do I—now.'

Kit looked at him curiously. 'How do you know?'

Marcus's mouth twisted self-derisively. 'Because I have one of his paintings hanging on my apartment wall. I sat there in my apartment all weekend—'

'We didn't come back to town until Saturday afternoon,' Kit reminded him.

Marcus gave her a scathing look. 'I sat there all weekend,' he repeated, 'when I suddenly realised that the painting I was staring at was by Tom McGuire. It was just too much of a coincidence for it not to have been painted by your father!'

Kit didn't even attempt to deny the connection—how could she? 'His paintings are considered a very sound investment nowadays—'

'I didn't buy the painting as an investment!' he replied. 'I've owned it for twelve or thirteen years now.'

She nodded. 'It's only the last ten years he's suddenly become quite famous—'

'Quite famous!' Marcus echoed with an incredulous note in his voice. 'Each of his paintings are worth thousands of pounds!'

'And do you know how old he was when he suddenly became famous?' she returned exasperatedly. 'Sixty-two,' she continued without waiting for him to answer. 'Before that he and my mother lived on the little they could make selling the odd painting and some of the vegetables my mother grows—in—in their huge—garden.' Her voice began to falter as the façade she had kept up so far this morning slowly began to crumble and disintegrate. 'It was a—a happy life,' she defended huskily. 'But it certainly wasn't—wasn't—' She simply couldn't go on any more, her throat clogged with the tears she was trying so hard not to shed.

She had tried so hard to appear normal this morning, to come to work as normal, to sit at her desk as normal, even to carry out this ridiculous conversation with Marcus as normal—when in reality her whole world felt as if it were falling apart. Every certainty, every stability in her life, suddenly no longer seemed that way...

*   *   *

She had travelled down to Cornwall on Saturday, totally ignorant of the bombshell that was about to be dropped on her.

'Kit!' her mother cried out excitedly, absolutely thrilled to see her getting out of the taxi, running over to hug her, and then promptly bursting into tears.

'Hey…' Kit said gently once she had paid off the taxi, looking affectionately at her tall, slender, still-beautiful mother.

Heather McGuire had been a noted beauty in her youth, with her long auburn hair and classical features. She was still a very striking woman.

She linked her arm with Kit's as the two of them strolled over to the cottage. 'I'm just so pleased to see you.' She beamed. 'Your father will be too,' she added with certainty.

And he was, taking Kit up in his arms and hugging her.

He was tall and handsome, his hair and beard snowy white now; his blue eyes twinkled at her merrily as he said, 'You're looking lovelier than ever, Kit; new boyfriend?'

'No,' she laughingly denied.

He arched white brows. 'Still hankering after that handsome boss of yours?'

'For all the good it's doing me,' she confessed, knowing she never had been able to keep secrets from her father.

'Come along in and let's all have a glass of wine before dinner,' her mother suggested happily, her tears dried now.

Kit hung back as her mother went off to get the glasses for their wine, looking concernedly at her father. 'What's wrong with Mummy?'

'Wrong?'

'Wrong,' Kit insisted, very aware of the fact that her father's voice sounded forced, that his eyes weren't quite meeting hers, or in fact twinkling any more.

'Why, nothing, darling—'

'Daddy,' she rebuked gently. 'I'm not a child any more, you know.'

'I do know.' He sighed wistfully. 'Long gone are the days when I could—'

'Daddy, please,' she encouraged, definitely knowing there was something wrong now from the way he was prevaricating.

Not that her mother wasn't always overjoyed to see her; she just didn't usually cry over it, had accepted long ago that Kit worked and lived in London, that she would come down every four to six weeks to see them. It had, in fact, only been three weeks since she'd last visited, so her mother's emotional outburst just now seemed totally out of character.

Her father hugged her to his side. 'We'll discuss it over dinner, all right, Pumpkin?' he told her gruffly.

No, it wasn't all right, but she knew her father too well to try and push him; he would explain when he was ready and not before.

And he had explained, both he and her mother...

But it wasn't an explanation she intended sharing with Marcus now, here in his office.

His anger this morning was one thing, something, she could deal with; his sympathy would be something else entirely!

'Which painting is it?' she asked, recovering her composure.

'"Tempest",' Marcus revealed. 'The young girl on the rocks? It's you, isn't it?'

'Yes,' she confirmed, knowing exactly which painting he was referring to, of a young girl, red hair swirling behind her, as she sat on the rocks looking out at a storm-tossed sea.

Kit had been thirteen when her father had painted her, no longer a child, but not quite a woman yet, either. That winter, some days she had been so angry with herself, the world, everything, that her only escape had been to go to the beach near their cottage, sit on the rocks, uncaring of how wet she became, and just allow herself to become a part of the stormy sea.

Her father had seen her there one day and captured her on canvas.

And it was incredible to think that Marcus had owned that particular painting for all this time...!

She gave a warm smile. 'It's probably now worth a hundred times what you paid for it.'

Intensity flared in the dark depths of Marcus's eyes. 'I have no intention of selling it.'

'It's a very sound investment.'

'I told you, I didn't buy it as an investment!' he came back impatiently.

'I was only—'

'Kit, I know what you were "only",' he cut in forcefully. 'And I don't appreciate it!'

Kit could see that he didn't. But if she were to have any pride left at all she had to try and keep up the barriers between them. And if that meant alienating Marcus, then that was what she would have to do.

Besides, she had other, much more pressing things to think about at the moment...

She met his gaze unblinkingly. 'I'm not sure this is the right moment to ask this—but do you think I could have a little longer for lunch today?'

'A little longer—!' Marcus looked momentarily non-plussed by this sudden change of subject, and then his gaze narrowed speculatively. 'Why?'

Her eyes widened. 'I don't think that is any of your business,' she told him stiffly. 'Of course, if it's going to interfere with anything here, then I—'

'It isn't,' he responded flatly. 'As it happens Lewis and I have to go to a meeting early this afternoon. I merely wondered if you were seeing someone for lunch.'

Kit felt perplexed now. This was the first she'd heard of any meeting arranged for this afternoon. 'Again, I don't really think that is any of your business…'

'You're asking me for extra time off—'

'I'll work later this evening to make up for it!' she came back heatedly, hands clenched at her sides. The extended lunch break she was requesting really wasn't up for negotiation—it was too important for that!

Besides, in the last six months she hadn't been off sick once, had never asked for any time off other than her allowed holiday. As far as she was concerned Marcus was being totally unreasonable.

'That won't be necessary,' he told her icily.

It might not be necessary, but she was going to do it anyway. No matter what the outcome of her lunch-time appointment…

It wasn't a meeting she was looking forward to, and that was without Marcus being so difficult about it.

'Kit?' Marcus's voice softened slightly, his gaze searching now on the paleness of her face.

She swallowed hard, straightening defensively. 'Will that be all, Mr Maitland?'

'No, it will not be all, damn it!' he barked once more, taking a determined step towards her to grasp her by her upper arms, once again taking in her businesslike appearance with obvious displeasure. 'You look totally ridiculous in that get-up.'

Her mouth tightened at his deliberately insulting tone. 'Thank you!'

'You know very well what I mean!'

'Do I?' Kit eyed him challengingly, very aware that she was playing with fire, but unable, at that moment—later might be a different matter!—to resist.

Besides, the mere touch of his hands, even when he was bad-tempered like this, had rekindled her yearning to be in his arms, to know the thrill of his lips on hers, to lose herself in the passion the two of them seemed to ignite in each other.

Some of that yearning must have shown in her eyes, because Marcus, giving a groan low in this throat, bent his head and his lips moved to possess hers.

Kit returned the kiss as all of the emotions of the last few days washed over her, losing herself in the fierceness of the desire that flared so intensely between them. Marcus's arms were about her now as he moulded the length of her body against his, making her fully aware of his arousal.

He felt so good to touch, his back hard and muscled against her restlessly caressing hands beneath his suit jacket, his warmth heating her body, her breasts aching heavily, her nipples hard and ultra-sensitive against his chest.

She had been waiting for this man all her life, it

seemed; that young girl on the rocks in her father's painting, who'd dreamed of the man she might one day fall in love with, who during the years since had waited for that man to appear—only to have him do so now, in the guise of Marcus Maitland.

How she loved this man! How she longed to just lie down beside him and make love with him, to become lost in the—

Kit looked up at Marcus unseeing as she suddenly found herself thrust away from him. 'What—?'

'Come in!' Marcus called out, his gaze not leaving hers.

Someone—Lewis, it seemed as the other man opened the door and entered the office—had knocked on the door, a knock Kit hadn't heard in her total awareness of Marcus. Her cheeks blushed scarlet as she saw the knowing look harden Marcus's eyes.

'I have the papers here I thought you should look at,' Lewis told Marcus slowly, obviously sensing the tension in the room as he looked at the two of them questioningly. 'But if you're busy, I can always come back later…?' He seemed aware that he had interrupted something—although, hopefully, not actually what that was!

'I was just leaving, anyway,' Kit assured him, deliberately avoiding meeting Marcus's eyes as she turned away.

'Kit…?' he called out as she reached the open door.

She stiffened, turning slowly back to look at him, wishing he would just let her escape.

'That extended lunch break you requested…'

'Yes?' she replied warily, very aware of Lewis as he

studied the papers in his hand in an effort to try looking as if he weren't listening to their conversation.

'It's fine with me,' Marcus told her.

She drew in a sharp breath, wanting to make a cutting reply back, but unwilling to add to Lewis's curiosity by doing so. 'Thank you,' she accepted tersely, at last able to escape to the relative sanctuary of her own office.

She had known it was going to be difficult to come in today and just continue working with Marcus, as if nothing had changed between them over the weekend. That was one of the reasons—despite what Marcus might have thought!—she had returned to her guise as efficient, prim Miss McGuire. But the fact that Marcus had kissed her in the way that he had showed he had no intention of forgetting the intimacy they had shared over the weekend. How much longer, Kit wondered miserably, would she be able to continue working for him...?

CHAPTER TWELVE

'KIT...isn't it?'

Kit stared at the woman sitting behind the wide oak desk, hoping the trembling of her legs wasn't visible as she stood on the thickly carpeted floor in front of that desk. The last thing she wanted was to appear in the least lacking in self-confidence.

'You asked to see me,' Catherine Grainger reminded at Kit's continued silence.

Yes, she had. She had telephoned Catherine Grainger's office first thing this morning; lunchtime was the only time the other woman was available to see her. But now that Kit was here she had no idea what she was going to say to her!

Her hands were clammy, she felt alternately hot and then cold—and she seemed to have forgotten how to talk!

The older woman gave an impatient sigh. 'I'm sure my secretary has already explained to you that I'm very busy today, so if you have something to say then I really wish you would get on with it—'

'My name is Catherine McGuire!' The words burst out starkly before Kit even had time to formulate them in her mind.

Catherine Grainger remained unmoved, her face hard and unyielding. 'I believe my secretary did mention that was the name of my one o'clock appointment, yes.'

'Doesn't that name mean anything to you?'

Catherine Grainger lifted elegant shoulders in dismissal. 'Should it?' she returned coolly.

Kit drew in a sharp breath, her face deathly pale now, her hands clenched tightly into fists at her sides. 'I'm your granddaughter!'

Catherine Grainger continued to look at her, her expression impassive, not showing so much as a flicker of her eyelids to demonstrate that what Kit had said meant anything to her.

Kit stared back, still amazed that this woman, so cold, so hard, could possibly be her mother's mother!

She had always known who her grandmother was, of course, had been told the truth by her parents at a very young age, after she had asked them why she didn't have grandparents like the other children at school. But actually coming face to face with her the previous weekend, knowing exactly who and what she was, had been something of a shock.

A shock, now she had been told the truth, Catherine Grainger didn't seem to share...

Catherine gave a gesture of acknowledgement. 'Yes,' she agreed.

It wasn't a question, or an exclamation, just a simple statement of fact!

Kit was startled. 'You already knew...?'

'I guessed. You look remarkably like your mother did at this age,' she explained unemotionally.

'You haven't even seen my mother since she was nineteen!' Kit exclaimed, stunned beyond measure that this woman had known all the time exactly who she was. And had said nothing...

'True,' Catherine Granger confirmed. 'But you're

still very like her to look at. The likeness was enough for me to—ask certain questions, in order to find out exactly who you were.'

Kit's eyes widened. 'Of whom?'

'Does that really matter?'

'What questions did you ask?' Kit persisted.

'Your surname was enough to tell me all that I needed to know.' Her grandmother's top lip turned back scornfully.

'And yet you said nothing?' Kit said incredulously.

Catherine Grainger's eyes narrowed icily. 'What was there for me to say? So you're the daughter of Heather and that man—'

'That man is my father!' Kit interjected. 'And he has a name. Tom McGuire,' she announced proudly.

Her grandmother's mouth thinned. 'He's old enough to be Heather's father, and your grandfather!'

Kit stared at her disbelievingly. 'And is that the only reason you objected to their relationship all those years ago? The reason you made my mother choose between the two of you?'

Heather had explained to her daughter that her own mother didn't approve of her choice of husband, that it had come to a choice between the two, and that Tom had easily won.

Having met Catherine Grainger at the weekend, and looking at her now, Kit could easily understand why Heather had chosen to be with the man she loved, and who loved her, rather than this cold, unemotional woman. What Kit couldn't understand was why Catherine had forced Heather to make that choice in the first place...

'Isn't that reason enough?' Catherine came back derisively.

'Not to me, no!' Kit denied.

Catherine gave a humourless laugh. 'I don't really think this is any of your business, do you?'

'None of my—!' Kit gasped disbelievingly. 'What sort of woman are you?'

Those grey eyes—like Kit's own, only hers were warm as velvet rather than cold as ice!—hardened glacially. 'Heather was nineteen years old, hardly more than a child herself—what did she know about love?'

'Enough for that love to have lasted twenty-eight years!' Kit told her grandmother triumphantly.

Catherine looked unimpressed. 'They're still together, then?'

'Of course they're still together!' Kit had wondered how she was going to feel when she confronted this woman today, but now she knew exactly how she felt—furiously angry! This was Catherine's own daughter they were talking about, a child this woman had presumably nurtured until she was nineteen years old. And yet, Catherine could have been talking about a stranger.

Catherine grimaced. 'More from luck than judgement, I'm sure.'

Kit could feel her emotions building. 'What absolute rubbish! If anything my parents love each other more now than they did twenty-eight years ago.'

'Love!' the other woman scorned.

Kit had once asked Heather why she hadn't tried to see her mother over the years, to try and make up the quarrel between them, to show Catherine that years later she was still happy with the man of her choice.

Her mother had looked bleakly unhappy as she had assured Kit that would never be possible.

Looking at Catherine's expression of contempt just at the mention of the word love, Kit could now understand her mother's reticence. Heather had already been hurt once; why put herself through the risk of a second rejection…?

'Yes—love,' Kit told her grandmother heavily. 'Something you obviously know nothing about!'

Kit had come here today because she had felt compelled to do so, because after talking with her parents at the weekend, and knowing who this woman was, she felt she owed it to Catherine.

'And you know absolutely nothing about me, Kit McGuire!' her grandmother spat the words.

'Then tell me! Explain to me why it is a mother disowns her own daughter, doesn't even see her for the next twenty-eight years, just because she dared to fall in love with a man her mother doesn't approve of! Because I certainly don't understand it. My mother would never do that to me,' Kit added with absolute certainty.

She didn't care about this for herself, had lived without a grandmother for the last twenty-six years, was sure she could live without one for the rest of her life. But she cared for her mother's sake…

Catherine gave a cynical laugh. 'No, I don't suppose innocently trusting Heather ever would.'

The heat flooded Kit's cheeks as she heard the contempt in Catherine's voice. 'My mother is seriously ill! She could die,' she explained in a pained voice, still too shocked by that knowledge herself to be able to soften or lessen the terrible enormity of what her parents had told her over the weekend.

Her mother had begun to have headaches a few months ago, which had become worse as time went on. A visit to a doctor was followed by one to a specialist, who diagnosed that those headaches were being caused by a brain tumour. A tumour that needed to be operated on straight away in order for Heather to stand any chance of living out the year.

Kit had cried brokenly when told the news, absolutely devastated at the seriousness of her mother's illness. But as far as she could see, that same news had elicited very little reaction from Catherine Grainger.

A nerve pulsed briefly in her grandmother's creamy cheek, there was a flicker of something in her eyes, though it was too brief for Kit to be able to tell what it was. But other than that, Catherine gave no outward response to the announcement.

'Did you hear me?' Kit snapped angrily. 'I said—'

'I heard you,' the older woman cut in softly.

'And?'

Catherine's chin lifted slightly. 'Exactly what is the nature of Heather's illness?'

'She has a brain tumour,' Kit told her frankly. 'They're going to operate on Thursday, but—' She broke off as her voice trembled emotionally. 'They're operating on Thursday,' she repeated flatly once she had herself back under control.

'Who is?' Catherine demanded.

'Does that really matter?' Kit sighed heavily. 'Don't worry, my father now has enough money to pay for the best, and that's what my mother has.'

Catherine stood up, looking haughtily down her nose at Kit. 'Does Heather know you've come to see me?'

'No,' Kit confirmed. 'In fact, my mother has no idea I've even met you.'

'I see.' Her grandmother breathed out slowly. 'Well, now that you've told me, what do you want me to do about it?'

Kit stared at her incredulously. 'Isn't it obvious? I thought you would want to know. Thought I owed it to you to tell you. So that—so that—'

'So that Heather and I can have some grand emotional reconciliation before her operation?' Catherine Grainger guessed. 'I hardly think so, Kit.'

Kit didn't understand her grandmother, couldn't relate to her at all. 'Why not?' she asked hesitantly.

Catherine stood ramrod straight before her, tall, elegant and imposing in a navy blue business suit and white silk blouse. 'Heather made her choice twenty-eight years ago. I no longer have a daughter.' Her expression hardened as she looked at Kit. 'Or a granddaughter. Even one apparently named after me.'

Kit was shocked into retaliation. 'Don't worry, I have absolutely no wish to be your granddaughter, either! In fact, I've done what I came here to do. Said what I came here to say. So now I can leave. Except...' She paused before turning to walk to the door.

'Yes?' Catherine replied stiffly.

Kit gave her a pitying glance. 'I would hate to be you, with no love in my life, no one who cares for me, or for me to care for. Oh, you're obviously very wealthy.' She looked around at the expensive furnishings of Catherine's office, evidence of her success in her business life. At the sacrifice of all else... 'But by being the way that you are, so hard and unforgiving, you've missed out on so much.'

'Having you as my granddaughter being one of them, I suppose?' Catherine shot back.

'Not at all,' Kit answered levelly. 'My mother is such a lovely woman, so undeserving of—of you, or her illness!'

Silver brows rose over cold grey eyes. 'Have you quite finished?'

Kit took a steadying breath. 'Yes, I've finished.'

'In that case—' Catherine looked quite deliberately in the appointment book on her desk top '—I have another meeting in two minutes.' She dismissed Kit with a wave of her hand.

'You really are very sad,' Kit finished.

'And you have taken up enough of my time for one day!' Catherine slammed back.

'So I have,' Kit accepted, adding nothing more, but turning on her heel and walking out of the office, closing the door carefully behind her.

She managed to stay calm as she walked down the corridor and into the lift, determined to hold onto her emotions until she was well away from here.

Away from Catherine Grainger. Her grandmother...

She didn't care for herself, had lived all these years without a grandmother, could live the rest of her life without one.

But what she didn't understand was how a mother could behave in that way.

Even knowing of Heather's illness, of the operation she would go through on Thursday, Catherine seemingly had no forgiveness in her, no softening of the resolve that had made her a stranger to her own daughter for the last twenty-eight years.

The only positive thing about this morning, as far as Kit could see, was that Heather knew nothing about her visit to Catherine, or of her mother's lack of compassion—

Kit came to a sudden halt as she stepped out of the lift and found herself face to face with both Marcus and Lewis.

A stunned Lewis.

And a *furious* Marcus!

CHAPTER THIRTEEN

'I HAVE another meeting in two minutes,' Catherine Grainger had told her so dismissively a few minutes earlier.

Obviously, that appointment was with Marcus and Lewis!

It had to be. It was just too much of a coincidence for it not to be.

'What the hell are you doing here?' Marcus exploded, apparently no more pleased to see Kit than she was to see him.

Kit moistened dry lips, but as quickly stopped the instinctive movement as she saw Marcus's eyes narrow ominously. 'I—I—' What could she say in answer to that question? How could she explain what had just taken place in Catherine Grainger's office?

'Would you leave us for a few minutes, Lewis?' Marcus instructed.

This was awful. Kit's worst nightmare. But how could she have known—how could she have guessed? Catherine Grainger hadn't said anything about *Marcus* being her next appointment, and Kit hadn't had any idea about whom he was going to meet today.

Which was curious in itself...

Of course, as Marcus's PA normally she dealt with all his appointments, had never known him to make his own arrangements like this before—with Catherine Grainger, of all people.

'Of course,' Lewis agreed, a little flustered, shooting Kit a questioning glance before moving away to stand over by the glass front doors of the building.

Marcus grasped hold of Kit's arm and pulled her away from the lifts and round the corner of the reception area, away from the curious eyes of both Lewis and the receptionist.

He released her from his grasp. 'Well?' he demanded forcefully, blue eyes boring into hers.

She swallowed hard. 'I—I—'

'You lied to me, Kit,' he said quietly, that nerve pulsing angrily in the rigid line of his tightly clenched jaw.

Her eyes widened in dismay as she realised what he must think: having found her here, he'd concluded that *she* must be passing on information to Catherine Grainger about his business transactions.

And who could blame him for thinking that? She *was* here. Clearly on her way down from Catherine's office. What other possible conclusion could Marcus come to but this?

Even so, she had to at least try to defend herself.

'No, Marcus, I didn't—'

'Oh, yes,' he interrupted, 'you did. Why, Kit? That's what I don't understand.' His expression was bleak. 'What did I ever do to you to make you do such a thing to me? Or are you just paying me back for the way Mike Reynolds behaved towards you—' he looked at her searchingly '—on the premise that all bosses are bastards?'

'But they aren't! You aren't!' Kit told him desperately. 'Marcus, you can't really believe I would behave like that? Do something so vicious?' She looked at him pleadingly, tears swimming in the smoky depths of her eyes.

'I don't know what to think any more,' he admitted, running an agitated hand through the dark thickness of his hair. 'And I really don't have the time to discuss this just now, either,' he said after a glance at his wrist-watch. 'But we will discuss it later, Kit. At length, in fact.'

Kit was sure that they would. But admitting to him now that Catherine Grainger was her grandmother wasn't likely to convince him that she wasn't his dis-loyal employee, now was it?

What a mess. A complete, unmitigated mess!

She looked at the floor. 'Maybe it would be better if I just went back to the office, packed up my things, and left...?' She really didn't want to do that, but in the circumstances she couldn't see what option she had.

'Oh, no, Kit,' Marcus assured her. 'You don't get away that easily. I want to know the who, what, when, where and why—most of all why!'

And she didn't have answers to any of those ques-tions!

'I have to go,' Marcus announced after another glance at his watch. 'But I shouldn't be too long,' he warned. 'In fact, I'm no longer sure this meeting is even necessary.'

Kit gave him a questioning look, a look he totally ignored as he walked away to join Lewis, the expres-sion on his face more than indicative of his mood.

And who could blame him? Kit thought sadly.

Lewis shot her another enquiring glance as she walked past the two men on their way to the lift, but it was one Kit chose to ignore, looking neither left nor right as she walked across the lobby, her head held high. Even though tears threatened to fall at any moment.

Her meeting with Catherine Grainger, in order to tell her of her mother's illness, had been a complete waste of time. Walking straight into Marcus on her way out had been nothing short of a disaster.

She had never felt so totally miserable in her life before, felt sure that Marcus, when he did return to the office, would demand answers, and when he got none would tell her to leave and never come back.

What other choice did he have? She looked guilty. Her behaviour appeared guilty. The fact that she wasn't was totally irrelevant.

Except…if she wasn't the one guilty of betraying Marcus, then who was?

'I thought I told you to stay at the office!' Marcus barked as soon as Kit opened her apartment door to him later that afternoon.

She knew exactly what he had said, appreciated why he had said it, but there was no way, having returned to the office, that she had been able to just sit there and wait for him to come back and sack her. So she had packed the few personal things she had about her office, left her set of keys on Marcus's desk, and made her weary way home.

She had known, after what he'd said earlier, that Marcus wouldn't let her get away that easily. But she'd decided that she would rather their confrontation took place on her home ground rather than in the formality of Marcus's office.

At least if he dismissed her here he couldn't actually have her thrown out of the building!

'I know what you told me, Marcus.' Blow 'Mr Maitland', she decided heavily. 'But I could see little point in my remaining there.'

Waiting for him to fire her!

'What's in the box?' she prompted as she noted the flat cardboard box he had beneath one arm.

'The rest of your things,' he stated flatly. 'Nothing of any importance. Aren't you going to invite me inside, Kit?'

She sighed, her hand clinging tightly to the door. 'Is there any point in my doing that?'

'Every point.' He gave a terse inclination of his head. 'Unless you want to have this conversation overheard by some of your neighbours?'

She would rather not be having this conversation at all, but, as she had known when she had left the office so precipitously that Marcus wouldn't just leave things as they were, it was a conversation she had been expecting to happen.

Even though she was no more prepared for it now than she had been earlier!

'Yes, do come in.' She stepped back to let him pass, almost able to feel the chill he emanated as he swept past her into the sitting-room beyond.

Kit followed more slowly. In order to put off the dreaded moment? There was little point in doing that. Reluctance to hear all the verbal abuse she was sure Marcus was going to rain down on her head? Possibly, she allowed. But mostly it was because she couldn't bear that look of contempt in his eyes now when he looked at her.

The cardboard box he had carried in now sat recriminatingly in the middle of the coffee table that stood in front of the sofa. Marcus looked tall and imposing as he stood in front of the unlit fireplace.

Unable to look at the accusation in his face any longer, Kit moved to pick up the box, opening its lid, the tears welling up as she looked at its contents: the fluffy yellow toy chick that had resided on top of her computer screen, her collection of pens—including the pot she kept them in!—that had stood on top of her desk, and lastly the card that had accompanied some flowers Marcus had sent to her a couple of months ago after he had concluded a very successful business deal, claiming her hard work had contributed immensely to that success. 'With many thanks, Marcus Maitland', the card read—as if she knew anyone else called Marcus, anyway!

'Nothing of any importance,' he had commented about the contents of the box. And perhaps to him that card wasn't important, just a thank you to an employee for a job well done, but Kit had kept it for secret sentimental reasons: it was something that Marcus had sent to her.

As she looked at it now that card brought her only pain.

The hand holding that card trembled slightly as she looked up at him. 'Didn't this mean anything to you?'

'Catherine Grainger wasn't involved in that particular deal. As you well know.'

Grainger International had never been interested in the acquisition of hotels, and this particular deal had involved Marcus buying a small chain of them, very exclusive, very up-market.

'I don't suppose there's any point in my saying I
didn't know?' She sighed, putting the card back in the
box and firmly closing the lid.

His mouth twisted scornfully. 'No point at all.'

'I didn't think so.'

'I'm glad to see you've discarded the disguise,'
Marcus said sardonically.

'It wasn't a disguise,' Kit protested, having changed
into denims and white tee shirt on arriving home earlier, her hair loose about her shoulders, contact lenses
in place now instead of her dark-framed glasses. She
was dressed in stark contrast to Marcus's formality, the
dark business suit, snowy white shirt and grey tie he
still wore.

'No?' Marcus taunted sceptically. 'I wonder…'

Kit was needled. 'I think that at the moment you're
adding two and two together and coming up with six!'

'Am I?' he countered. 'Then why don't you enlighten me as to what two and two really add up to?'
He moved over to the armchair, sitting down to look
up at her with expectancy.

What was the point when he had already judged her,
tried her, and found her guilty?

She took a deep breath. 'I know meeting me as I
came down from a meeting with Catherine Grainger
looked bad—'

'"Looked bad"?' he repeated, sitting forward in the
chair. 'It *was* bad, Kit,' he stated. 'And damning!'

'But only if—if—' She broke off.

She had decided, as she'd waited for Marcus to turn
up on her doorstep, that she had no choice but to tell
him the truth about her relationship with Catherine—
mainly on the basis that her grandmother could well

have already told him that, anyway!—and the real reason for which Kit had been to see her. But actually doing it, she was discovering, was something else entirely.

Once Kit had admitted to Marcus her connection with Catherine, she would then have to go on and tell him about her own mother, about how ill she was, about how Kit had pleaded with Catherine to go and see her daughter, to heal the breach between them before—before—

The seriousness of her mother's illness was still so raw to her, so devastating, that if she once began to talk about it she knew she would start crying and never stop!

Kit swallowed hard, her throat already clogged with tears. 'What did Catherine Grainger tell you about my visit to her?'

Marcus gave a humourless smile. 'You really think I asked her?'

Kit's eyes widened incredulously. 'Are you telling me that you didn't?'

'Of course I didn't!' He stood up, his size seeming to fill the room. 'Isn't it bad enough that my PA has been passing the woman confidential information, without giving her the satisfaction of gloating over it?' His eyes were so dark now they looked almost black.

'But—but—didn't she mention it either?' Kit gasped, having been sure that Catherine would very much enjoy telling Marcus about Kit's visit, if not the actual reason.

'No.'

Kit stared at Marcus, not quite open-mouthed, but not far from it. 'Are you telling me that the two of you went through the whole of your meeting without so much as mentioning the fact that I had been there a few minutes earlier?'

'I'm not telling you anything any more, Kit,' Marcus grated. 'You no longer work for me, remember?'

She inwardly flinched at the starkness of that statement. It was one thing knowing it, something else entirely when put into words.

'If you really must know, Kit,' Marcus went on harshly, 'I didn't ask Catherine Grainger, and she didn't volunteer the information, because after seeing you there I had no reason to continue with the meeting; Lewis offered to go up alone and cancel it.'

She gave a dazed shake of her head. 'I don't understand.'

'I'd grown tired of the game, had decided it was time to confront Catherine. Meeting you there cancelled out any need I had to do that.' He paused. 'I trusted you, Kit.'

Her breath caught in her throat at the total disillusionment in his tone. 'I thought you would have talked to Catherine, that she would have told you—! It never occurred to me—' she broke off, totally unsure as to what to do next. 'Marcus, I know you aren't going to believe me, but I'm not your mole!'

His mouth twisted mirthlessly. 'You're right—I don't believe you!'

She had an ache in her chest that was like no other pain she had ever known. Was it really possible for a heart to break? It certainly felt like it!

She took a step towards him. 'Marcus, please—'

'Please what?' He stood only inches away from her now as he towered over her ominously. 'Do you know the worst of this as far as I'm concerned, Kit? I actually liked you,' he said bitterly.

Liking was better than nothing, she supposed. Although Marcus had used the past tense...

'I wanted you, too,' he continued candidly, his dark gaze fixed on the trembling of her mouth now. 'I still do!' he muttered self-disgustedly. Then he reached out, pulled her into his arms and his mouth claimed hers.

It was a kiss of anger, of sheer, frustrated fury, his mouth hard and unyielding against hers, bending her to his will, with absolutely no allowance given to her feelings.

Kit didn't fight him, at that moment had no strength left in her to fight anything or anyone.

Finally Marcus wrenched his mouth from hers. He held her mere inches away from him, his face a mask of emotion as he stared down at her.

She loved this man. How she loved him!

His expression softened slightly. 'How could you do it, Kit?' His voice was flat now, his anger abating.

She shook her head. 'I didn't.'

He closed his eyes briefly. 'Don't lie to me! After the shock I've already received today, I don't think I can take any more of your lies!'

She drew in a sharp breath, more hurt than she cared to think about. 'I'm not lying, Marcus. Not now or in the past,' she told him quietly. 'I know you don't be-lieve me. But maybe when the betrayals continue after I've left the company, then you'll know I'm telling the truth.' That was her only hope.

She knew the evidence against her was damning, that to Marcus there could be only one explanation. But Kit also knew that if she had told him the truth about her relationship to Catherine Grainger it wouldn't have helped convince him that she hadn't betrayed him. The woman was her grandmother, for goodness' sake! Only finding the real culprit was ever going to do that.

Marcus made a frustrated movement. 'I think I can forgive anything but the lies, Kit.'

'But there's nothing to forgive—'

'Stop it. Just stop it!' He groaned low in his throat before pulling her back into his arms, his mouth once again taking possession of hers.

But his kiss was no longer angry as his mouth explored hers with searching thoroughness. His hands moved restlessly down the length of her spine, cupping her thighs to pull her against the increasing hardness of his body.

Despite everything he believed—in spite of everything he believed!—Marcus still wanted her!

Kit sobbed low in her throat as she gave herself up to the love she felt for this man, to the desire he obviously felt for her. For the moment it was enough. It had to be. Because there was nothing else.

Her arms moved up as her hands grasped his shoulders, feeling his tension beneath her fingertips, before she moved to entwine her fingers in the dark thickness of the hair at his nape. She felt his quiver of pleasure as she touched him there, his mouth moving erotically against hers now, the tip of his tongue searching on her bottom lip, her top lip, before moistly entering her.

Kit felt her senses soar, her body engulfed in sudden heat, straining against his as she wished herself a part of him.

'Kit…!' he whispered as his mouth left hers to travel the arched length of her throat. 'You taste so good!'

he murmured achingly, his lips and tongue now searching the hollows of her throat.

His hands were hot against her flesh now as he explored beneath her tee shirt, holding her arms above
her head as he peeled it from her body, his eyes dark
as he looked down at the thrusting softness of her
breasts in their lacy white bra and then back up to her
flushed face.

Kit held his eyes as she stepped back to slowly reach
behind her and release the catch to her bra, sliding the
straps from her shoulders to throw the garment to one
side.

Marcus froze, his gaze once again shifting to her
breasts, bare now to his scrutiny, their rosy tips firm
and aroused.

'You're beautiful…!' he exclaimed, then, moving
forward, his head bent and he slowly, oh, so slowly,
took one pouting nipple into his mouth.

Kit's legs buckled beneath her as she looked down
at his dark head against her creamy softness, moaning
low in her throat as his tongue lathed damply against
the rosy tip of her breast, her fingers digging tightly
into the hard strength of his shoulders as she clung to
him to stop herself falling.

Heat. There was so much heat in her body that she
felt as if she were on fire, the flames centred between
her thighs, that not even her increasing dampness there
could put out.

Marcus's hand moved to cup the breast he'd kissed
and sucked so pleasurably, the soft pad of his thumb
continuing that caress against the hardened nipple as
he turned the attention of his mouth to its twin.

Kit's legs really did give way as dual pleasure ripped

through her body. Marcus followed her down onto the carpeted floor, raising his head to look down to where one large hand still cupped her breast. Then his heated gaze returned to her face as he slowly moved his thumb across the sensitivity of her dampened nipple, holding her eyes as he bent his head to lick that rosy tip once more.

She couldn't breathe, the warmth between her thighs intensifying to an unbearable degree, ripples of pleasure building within her, her eyes widening as that pleasure began to overflow. The orgasm that ripped through her body seemed to last for ever and ever as Marcus kept her nipple in his mouth, and his hand moved down between her thighs so that he could feel the rippling convulsions of her deep satisfaction.

'Marcus!' Kit cried heatedly, her fingers digging into his shoulders now. 'Oh, Marcus!' she groaned brokenly, burying her face against his chest as she slowly began to come back down to earth.

What had just happened to her was completely unprecedented, like nothing she had ever known before, a total loss of control that had left her weak and trembling.

Marcus's hand moved to smooth the hair back from the dampness of her face, his expression once again guarded as he looked down at her flushed cheeks. 'I could take you right now,' he told her evenly. 'Could take the rest of your clothes from your body and take you again and again.'

'Yes,' she confirmed huskily.

'But I'm not going to.'

She swallowed hard, a stillness stealing over her as

she sensed distance moving over and into him. 'Why not?'

He drew in a shuddering breath, giving her one last intense look before rolling away from her and getting to his feet, his back turned towards her.

After only a moment's hesitation, Kit took advantage of his turned back to pull her tee shirt back on, aware that her breasts still thrust barely against the thinness of the material, but needing that barrier nonetheless, very aware of the intense satisfaction she had found only seconds ago in his arms. And the fact that Marcus hadn't reached that same completion.

He turned back suddenly, his face pale but his expression dark. 'Why not?' he repeated harshly. 'Because that would make me no better than Mike Reynolds, that's why not!' He thrust his hands into his trouser pockets.

Kit gasped. 'But you're nothing like Mike Reynolds—'

'No, I'm not,' he agreed. 'And I'll never give you the excuse to say that I am.'

'What happened just now—what happened to me—none of that was like Mike Reynolds, either,' she assured him with sincerity. 'Besides, I no longer work for you, remember?' She felt a chill as she repeated his earlier comment.

Marcus looked at her for several long seconds, and then he gave a determined shake of his head. 'I have to go.'

Sudden tears blurred Kit's vision. Biting down painfully on her bottom lip, she willed herself not to beg him to stay, much as she wanted to. Much as she wanted to once again lose herself in his arms, to take him with her this time.

'I have to go,' Marcus repeated, turning and striding from the room, the door to her apartment closing with controlled violence seconds later.

But Kit's control was completely shattered and she allowed the tears to fall hotly down her cheeks, having no doubts this time that the crushing pain she could feel in her chest *was* her heart breaking...!

CHAPTER FOURTEEN

'HE JUST came here and sacked you?' Penny looked at her disbelievingly.

Kit was loath to tell her flatmate what else had happened when Marcus had come here a couple of hours ago; after all, she did have some pride. Even if that pride completely deserted her whenever Marcus was around!

But Kit had had to give Penny some sort of explanation for the way she'd looked when her friend had arrived home a short time ago; there was just no hiding the puffy redness of her eyes or the deathly paleness of her cheeks.

'He felt he was justified, Penny—'

'Just because he saw you leaving Grainger International?' her friend fumed angrily. 'He can't do that! I'm sure there are laws to say that he can't just sack you without notice—'

'But he has. And he did,' Kit said flatly, one of her hands agitatedly pleating the material of her tee shirt. 'Penny, it really doesn't matter,' she pleaded wearily as her friend still looked outraged. 'There's no way I could go on working in the office with him anyway when he believes I've betrayed him.'

'But why didn't you tell him the truth?' Penny frowned at her frustratedly. 'Surely he would have to believe you—'

'If I were to tell you that I'm not the one leaking

154

confidential information, but that I was just visiting Catherine Grainger because she's my grandmother, would you believe me?' Kit reasoned; she had never made any secret of that fact to Penny, the two women having been friends for years.

'Well, of course, I—' Penny broke off, a perplexed frown marring her brow now. 'Maybe... But then again, maybe not,' she conceded slowly.

'You see,' Kit said sadly.

'It does sound—a little damning,' Penny allowed with a pained wince.

'A little!' Kit echoed bitterly.

'Don't you have enough—upset, going on in your life at the moment, with your mother's illness, without this?' Penny asked with genuine concern.

'Again, Marcus knows nothing about that,' Kit admitted.

'That isn't the point!' her friend exclaimed. 'And to think I actually liked the man!'

'So did I.' Kit sighed. 'But it's not—' She broke off as the telephone rang, giving Penny a grateful smile as her friend moved to answer the call, turning away to stare sightlessly out of the window, still trying to come to terms with the fact that Marcus had gone completely from her life.

But surely he had to realise at some time that she had been telling him the truth? Surely the next time one of his business deals was sabotaged...? But perhaps the real culprit was intelligent enough to realise that, and would cut their losses before that happened? It was what she would do. If she really had been the traitor...

'What do you want?' Penny demanded, turning to raise her groomed eyebrows at Kit.

Kit immediately tensed, at once dreading—and hoping!—that the caller might be Marcus. But maybe if it was he had already realised he had made a mistake? Maybe—

'Well, she doesn't want to talk to you!' Penny told the caller. 'Haven't you already done enough damage?' she added angrily. 'Kit already has enough to worry about at the moment without being falsely accused by you— Why should I tell you?' Penny exclaimed. 'Oh, give me a break! You have to be the most arrogant man I have ever met in my life! You don't think—! Listen, buster,' Penny continued furiously, 'I'm making it my business, okay?'

Kit had got to her feet as soon as she'd realised it was Marcus, but Penny's side of the conversation held her frozen with dismay.

'I'm glad we understand each other,' Penny went on heatedly. 'For the record, Kit is so honest she even drove back to a supermarket once because she realised she hadn't paid for the newspaper she was reading as she went through the checkout! You're right—it is a waste of time—mainly mine!' Penny fumed. 'And to think, I actually liked you! My only consolation is that you are going to feel like a complete idiot when you finally realise Kit had nothing to do with this!'

Kit was grateful for her friend's championing of her, but it was clear from Penny's reaction to Marcus's responses that it was getting her nowhere.

'I've already told you no,' Penny stated with force. 'She's upset enough already without having you start on her again. Oh, get lost,' she yelled, before slamming the receiver back down in its cradle. 'Arrogant bastard!' she muttered, her face tight with anger when she turned back to Kit.

Kit gave a wan smile. 'I sincerely hope that wasn't our landlord offering to lower our rent!'

Penny grimaced, some of the tension starting to leave her body. 'Very funny!' She smiled ruefully. 'Can you believe the arrogance of that man?'

'Yes,' Kit said flatly. 'But did you ever find out why he was calling?'

Penny pulled a face. 'He said he wanted to talk to you.'

Kit frowned. 'What about?' It was obvious from what she had been able to hear that Marcus hadn't changed his mind about her guilt.

Her friend hesitated. 'He didn't say. Well…to be strictly honest—I didn't give him the chance to.' She put her hand to her mouth self-consciously. 'I guess I told him, didn't I…?'

Kit gave a ghost of a smile. 'I guess you did.'

Penny looked upset. 'I'm sorry—did you want to talk to him? It's just that I can't stand the way he's hurt you. You're already so worried about your mother that you didn't need all this on top of it.'

'No, I didn't want to talk to him,' Kit confirmed. 'He probably just wanted to insult me some more, anyway.'

'Probably,' Penny agreed. 'Can you believe him just phoning up here after what he did to you this afternoon?'

And Penny wasn't even completely aware of what Marcus had done to her that afternoon…!

Kit still blushed to think about the time she had spent

in his arms, of Marcus's response to her, seemingly
against all his instincts, as if he totally despised his
own weakness.

Which he probably did.

She straightened determinedly. 'Let's forget all
about Marcus Maitland and make something for dinner.' It was Roger's evening for going to the gym, so
Penny wouldn't be meeting him until much later.

To give Penny her due, she fell in with this plan
with a light heart, although when it actually came to
eating the spaghetti bolognese, neither woman really
had much appetite, picking at the food, enjoying the
red wine that accompanied it more.

In fact, Kit was sure it was a relief to both of them
when the doorbell rang to announce Roger's arrival an
hour later.

'Would you like us to stay in with you this evening…?' Penny paused on her way to answer the door.
The engaged couple were due to go to a later evening
showing of a recently released film. 'I really don't like
the idea of just leaving you here alone.'

Kit smiled her gratitude, but shook her head. 'To be
honest, I think I would quite enjoy a little time to myself.' If only to try to come to terms with the fact that
she was never again going to see the man that she
loved. Marcus…

'If you're sure…?' Penny didn't look convinced.

'Positive,' Kit assured her bravely, standing up to
begin clearing away the plates for their meal.

Plates she almost dropped as she turned and found
herself face to face with Marcus as he stood in the open
doorway.

'What do you want?' she blurted out rudely, too shocked to be anything else.

His mouth twisted humourlessly. 'I'm getting a little tired of people asking me that this evening!' He gave a pointed glance back at Penny as she stood in the hallway behind him.

'Then maybe you shouldn't keep barging in unannounced,' Penny came back tartly. 'Sorry, Kit, but he just walked in.' Her flatmate gave her an apologetic grimace before once again turning to glare at Marcus.

Kit put the plates she held carefully back down on the tabletop—before she dropped them from her suddenly shaking hands!

Telephoning her was one thing, but arriving unannounced on her doorstep like this was—as Penny had already pointed out so succinctly!—totally unexpected.

Marcus looked at her under hooded lids. 'Could I talk to you, Kit? Alone,' he added.

'You really do have a nerve—'

'It's all right, Penny,' Kit cut in reassuringly, though her hands were tightly clenched at her sides. 'I know you have to go out, and I'm sure Mr Maitland won't be staying long.'

'If you're sure…?' Penny looked far from convinced that leaving Kit alone with Marcus was the right thing to do.

But Kit knew that her friend had nothing to worry about; one look at Marcus's face, his expression and dispassionate eyes, and she knew that whatever he had come here to say it had nothing to do with apologising to her, either for his mistaken accusations, or for making love to her.

'I'm sure.' She gave Penny an encouraging smile.

Penny smiled back before turning to give Marcus a hard stare. 'Just don't upset her any more than she already is,' she warned.

'I'll try not to,' he replied. 'And by the way,' he went on as Penny turned to leave, 'I quite liked you too.'

Penny gave him a look that could kill before leaving the room and closing the door softly behind her.

Leaving a painful tension between Kit and Marcus. At least—it was painful to her! She doubted Marcus felt any such awkwardness.

But as the silence continued between them the tension just seemed to get more intense to Kit, so much so that in the end she couldn't stand it any longer. 'Well?' she prompted.

'Well what?' Marcus returned.

Kit raised her hands in frustration. 'You were the one who telephoned me,' she reminded him. 'You're also the one visiting my apartment.'

An apartment he had frequented little more than three hours ago. Although there was no memory of that, it seemed, in his coldly opaque eyes.

'So I am,' he agreed. 'When I spoke to Penny earlier she—well, she gave me the impression that there's something else going on in your life other than—our argument, earlier today…?'

'You have no idea!' she mocked his arrogance. 'Besides, it wasn't an argument; you sacked me!'

His mouth tightened. 'I accepted your resignation, effective imm—'

'That's a lie!' she defended indignantly.

'You cleared your desk and left your keys—'

'Only because you had already made it perfectly obvious that you were going to make me do that anyway!'

'Whatever. The outcome was effectively the same.'

Kit noticed how handsome he looked in the casual black trousers he wore with an open-necked shirt.

'The outcome may have been,' she said, dragging herself back to reality. 'But there is a vast difference between my resigning and your sacking me!'

Marcus quirked a challenging brow. 'Worried I might not give you a good reference?'

Her eyes flared angrily. 'Not in the least,' she snapped. 'Now would you just state your reason for being here and then leave?'

'What's going on, Kit?'

She started nervously. 'Going on...?' she delayed.

'Penny said you were upset—'

'Well, of course I'm upset—I've just lost my job!' Kit reminded him.

'That isn't it,' Marcus said slowly.

'Why isn't it?' she defended. 'You may have so much money lying around that being out a job wouldn't bother you, but some of us need to pay rent and eat occasionally!'

He looked at her steadily for several long seconds, and then he slowly gave another shake of his head. 'That isn't it,' he repeated firmly. 'What happened over the weekend, Kit?' he prompted astutely. 'And don't tell me nothing did—because I won't believe you.'

'What's new?'

His mouth tightened, his eyes dark now. 'I know you're trying to annoy me into walking out of here, Kit, but it isn't going to work,' he told her with certainty. 'I want to know the reason behind Penny's earlier remark—she's a worthy champion, by the way,' he acknowledged sardonically, 'and I'm not leaving until I know what's going on!' As if to add weight to this statement he sat down in one of the armchairs.

Kit watched him silently for several seconds, and then she gave in. 'My mother isn't very well, that's all,' she revealed.

All? It was everything! If anything should happen to her mother—if she didn't come through the operation on Thursday—

But she mustn't think like that, Kit immediately admonished herself. She had to be positive for both her mother's and her father's sakes.

'As in?' Marcus was once again studying her intently.

'As in not very well,' she repeated. 'It's really none of your business, is it?'

'I care about you, Kit—'

'Oh, please!' she derided.

'But I do care, damn it!' He stood up, suddenly towering over her. 'I don't want to,' he admitted, 'but that doesn't change the fact that I do!'

Kit looked up at him, seeing only implacable anger in his face, his eyes cold with the fury of his admission. 'Don't let it worry you, Marcus,' she taunted. 'It's probably just like a summer cold, rather uncomfortable for a few days, but quickly gone!'

'Very funny,' he rasped coldly. 'So you aren't going to tell me?'

'I just did.' She sighed wearily. 'My mother isn't very well, I'm naturally worried about her. End of story.'

'Somehow I don't think so,' he said slowly.

Kit tried to look unconcerned. 'Think what you like—you usually do, anyway! Now, if you wouldn't mind...' She looked in the direction of the door.

Marcus didn't move. 'The reason I telephoned earlier was because I had received a call from Desmond Hayes, inviting the two of us out to a celebration dinner with him and his wife tomorrow evening.'

Her face brightened. 'The two of them are back together, then?'

'It would seem so,' Marcus confirmed distantly.

'I'm so glad! For Desmond's sake,' she exclaimed warmly.

'Yes,' Marcus agreed. 'Well?'

Well, what? He couldn't seriously expect that she would calmly go out to a dinner that included him with the way things stood between the two of them?

'I'm afraid not,' she told him quietly.

'I did tell Desmond that when he called to make the invitation, but he still insisted I ask you anyway,' Marcus said off-handedly.

Kit's hands tightened at the pain he deliberately inflicted by letting her know he had no desire to spend any more time in her company, either. 'Well, now you've asked me,' she said flatly.

'Yes,' he agreed curtly.

'Was there something else?'

'No,' he answered after another short pause, standing up. 'Nothing else. I'll give Desmond and Jackie your good wishes tomorrow evening, then, shall I?'

'Do that,' she agreed.

'Fine,' he bit out briskly. 'I'll say goodnight, then.'

'Yes,' Kit acknowledged dully.

'Kit—'

'Will you please just go?' she snapped at him, her self-control dangerously on the edge of cracking wide open.

He drew in a harsh breath. 'There's something you aren't telling me—'

'There's nothing I need to tell you!' she dismissed hurriedly. 'You're not even my employer any more!'

'No,' he acknowledged heavily.

As if that bothered him. Which Kit was sure it didn't. And they could hardly work together again anyway after the intimacies they had shared this afternoon.

'Okay, Kit, I'm going,' he accepted when she continued to look at him challengingly. 'But I will find out what's going on.'

She gave a disbelieving laugh. 'I have no idea how!' she responded. 'Or why it should interest you,' she added as he continued to look at her with that implacable expression.

'You might be surprised.'

'I doubt it,' she said. 'Now if there was nothing else…?' She folded her arms and looked him square in the face.

No matter what effort of will it cost her to do it! And it took a lot, his being here again at all giving her self-control a battering.

'For the moment,' he allowed. 'But I have a feeling that I'll be back.'

Her chin rose defensively. 'And I have a feeling that I'll be busy if you are!'

He gave a humourless smile. 'Then I'll just have to wait until you aren't busy, won't I?' He turned and left the apartment.

Kit swayed where she stood, totally overwhelmed— and confused—by this second visit from Marcus today.

CHAPTER FIFTEEN

'GET in.'

Kit peered into the interior of the car that had pulled to a halt at the pavement beside her as she waited for her taxi to arrive, her eyes widening with dismay as she saw it was Marcus sitting behind the wheel of the Jaguar—which she should already have recognized!

And maybe she would have done if she weren't already so agitated that she couldn't think straight!

'No, thank you.' She straightened, turning purposefully to look down the road for her taxi.

'Kit.' Marcus had got out of his car now, dark glasses hiding his eyes as he looked across at her over the low roof. 'I'll drive you to the clinic.'

She gave him a startled look. 'How did you—? You said you would find out,' she acknowledged with resignation. 'I don't think so, thank you.'

She was already worried enough. Her mother and father had arrived at the clinic the previous afternoon, and Kit had spent most of the evening there with them. Her father had stayed at the clinic overnight in preparation for the operation later this morning...

Her eyes filled with the ready tears that never seemed to be far away at the moment. 'Go away, Marcus,' she choked. 'I really can't deal with any arguments today.'

'You won't have to,' he said soothingly, having

moved around to her side of the car. 'I promise I won't even speak if you don't want me to.' He held the door open for her as he helped her into the passenger seat.

'Oh, yes?' Kit gave him a disbelieving look.

'Yes,' he confirmed evenly. 'Let me help you with that.' He took the seat belt out of her hand as she fumbled with it, one of his hands lightly brushing against her breast as he pushed the catch into the fastener.

Kit immediately felt the heat that washed over her. Even now, when she was so worried about her mother? It would appear so.

She shook her head, knowing he couldn't help but be aware of her response. 'Marcus, I really don't think I can deal with you today,' she told him pleadingly.

'I told you, you won't have to.' He gave her a re-assuring glance as he got into the car beside her.

'But what about my taxi?' she wailed.

Marcus shrugged unconcernedly. 'He'll find another fare.'

'Yes, but—I'm keeping you from your work,' she protested. 'Or is Lewis holding the fort today?'

His mouth tightened. 'Something like that.'

'But—oh, never mind.' She could see that her protests were getting her precisely nowhere; if he wanted to waste his morning on her, then that was up to him. 'Just drive me to the clinic, if that's what you really want to do.'

'It's one of the things I really want to do,' he affirmed. 'Most of the others are probably out of the question!' His meaning was more than obvious as his gaze lingered on her mouth.

Kit gave him a baffled look. 'I don't understand you;

you think I gave details of your business deals to Catherine Grainger!'

'Do I?' he shot back, switching on the engine, putting the car in gear, and driving off. 'If I do, it doesn't seem to have made much difference, does it?'

Difference to what? Kit wanted to know. To the fact that he was here? Or something else…?

'How did your dinner go with Desmond and Jackie last night?' She deliberately changed the subject onto something she could understand.

'Very well. Although they both expressed their disappointment that you weren't able to be there. Several times.'

Kit looked down. 'I'm sorry.'

'It's okay.' Marcus reached out and squeezed her tightly clenched hands. 'I understand the reason for your refusal now.'

'But I wouldn't have come even if it wasn't for—wasn't for—'

'Everything will work out, Kit,' he assured her determinedly. 'Your mother's surgeon is the best in his field—'

'How do you know? Never mind.' She knew Marcus well enough by now to realise that what he wanted to know, he would find out.

'Yes, he is,' she agreed. 'But he's still only given my mother a fifty-fifty chance of survival.' Tears filled her eyes again as she thought of her beautiful mother and all she would have to endure over the next few hours.

'We'll be there in a few minutes, Kit,' Marcus said quietly.

Kit still had no real idea of why Marcus was here, but a part of her was very glad that he was. Both she and her father were very supportive in front of her mother, but once alone…! The two of them would have need of Marcus's strength.

'I know.' She wiped the tears from her cheeks. 'It's just—just—'

'I know, Kit,' he gently interjected. 'But whatever happens I'll be there for you, okay?'

But why would he? What was he doing here at all? Kit didn't know the answer to either of those questions, and she was too emotionally upset at the moment to even try to find the answers.

'Now we have to be strong for your mother and father—yes?' he prompted as he parked the car outside the clinic.

He was right, Kit knew he was right, that she had to at least try to present a façade of cheerfulness once with her parents.

'Yes,' she agreed, slowly getting out of the car, drawing in deeply controlling breaths as she looked across at the one-storey private clinic where her mother lay awaiting her fate.

Marcus locked the car before taking a firm hold of her elbow. 'I'll be right here, Kit.'

She no longer questioned his presence, it was enough that he was here. Nothing else mattered—not his accusations, the fact that she no longer worked for him. He was here…

'Kit, before we go in, there's something I—' Marcus ventured. He broke off, at last removing those dark sunglasses. 'I wasn't exactly truthful with you earlier,' he confessed.

She gave him a puzzled glance. 'No?'

'Lewis isn't holding the fort—because as of nine o'clock this morning he no longer works for me!'

Her confusion deepened; what possible interest could it be to her now whether or not Lewis still worked for him? 'I don't understand,' she replied.

'I know you don't,' he responded. 'And now isn't the time for us to talk about it. But for what it's worth, I'm sorry I ever doubted you. I know that isn't enough after the things I said to you, the things I did, but—I really am very sorry.'

The last two days had been awful, and she had barely slept last night, could hardly think straight now, let alone understand why Marcus was apologizing to her.

'Don't worry about it now.' Marcus moved to run a gently caressing hand down the paleness of her cheeks. 'I still have no idea what you were doing at Catherine Grainger's office on Tuesday, but—I'll explain what I do know later, okay?'

Later. When they would all know one way or another how her mother had fared.

Kit had heard nothing from Catherine Grainger since their meeting. Not that she had expected to after the cold response she had received from the other woman on Tuesday. But she still couldn't help feeling hurt on her mother's behalf.

'Fine,' she told Marcus distractedly, eager to visit her mother now.

She saw her father almost immediately as they approached her mother's room, standing outside in the corridor, as handsome as ever, looking very much like a well-matured version of the actor Donald Sutherland.

Her heart ached at the defeated expression on her father's face, his wide shoulders slumped, although his face lit up as soon as he saw Kit, blue eyes warming with paternal love as he took her in a bear hug.

'Everything's fine,' he said as she looked up at him anxiously. 'The doctor is with her now, and then we can all go in.' He turned to include Marcus in his re-assuring smile, although there was a question in his eyes as he turned back to Kit.

'Marcus Maitland.' Marcus was the one to introduce himself to the older man, holding out his hand. 'It's a pleasure to meet you, Mr McGuire. Although I obvi-ously wish it could have been under happier circum-stances,' he added apologetically.

'Mr Maitland.' Kit's father returned the handshake, the two men obviously sizing each other up.

Not that Kit could tell from either of their expres-sions what conclusions they had come to, but for the moment that didn't matter, either. 'How's Mummy?' she prompted concernedly.

Her father grimaced. 'Tired. Frightened. Most of all worried about the two of us if—if—'

'She's going to be fine,' Kit told him determinedly, at the same time feeling her hand taken in a firm grasp. Marcus squeezed it reassuringly, and she had to blink back fresh tears as she turned to look at him.

And then she had to blink rapidly again—not only to clear those tears, but also to make sure her eyes weren't deceiving her as something else, some move-ment, caught and held her attention.

Walking down the carpeted corridor towards them, her face coolly composed, was Catherine Grainger!

Tall. Elegantly beautiful in the perfectly tailored black suit and white blouse. Her expression haughty. Grey eyes icily remote.

But she was here…!

'What the—?' Kit's father gasped at her side, his face stricken as he recognized the woman walking so purposefully towards them. 'What's she doing here?' he demanded. 'How—?'

'It's my fault, Daddy,' Kit told him quickly, her shoulders tensing at the enormity of what she had done. 'I went to see her on Tuesday to tell her about Mummy.' She didn't even glance at Marcus as she felt his hand tighten painfully about hers as the significance of what she had just said sank in; her attention was all centred on her father as he still stared disbelievingly at his mother-in-law.

The older woman came to a halt a few feet away from them, her expression wary now. 'Tom,' she greeted tersely.

'Catherine,' he returned guardedly.

'How is she?' Catherine Grainger enquired in her brisk, no-nonsense voice, seeming to have decided to ignore the fact that Kit and Marcus were there too.

'Resigned but determined too,' Kit's father answered economically.

Catherine nodded, as if she would have expected little else from a daughter of hers. 'Can I see her?'

'That depends,' Kit's father said slowly. 'On what you intend saying to her if you do see her,' he added as Catherine raised haughtily questioning brows.

Kit could see some of the arrogant self-confidence leaving that handsome face as her grandmother paused uncertainly, as if aware that so much rested on what she said next.

'To be honest, Tom...' Catherine finally spoke uncertainly '...I have no idea! Except...I have to say something.'

His expression softened slightly. 'That would appear to be a start!'

Kit found herself glancing at Marcus as he studied Catherine. Then he looked at Kit.

Although she had no time to even acknowledge that questioning look as the surgeon came out of her mother's room, all of them turning to look at him anxiously.

'You can all go in for a few minutes now,' the tall, middle-aged man informed them. 'Although, as we've already given Mrs McGuire her pre-med, you may find her a little sleepy.'

Kit felt the hand still holding hers increase its pressure. Turning to look at Marcus, she saw his own gaze now fixed on the woman he could see inside the hospital room.

Kit's mother...

And Kit could see exactly what Marcus must now be seeing. It was as if Heather were the missing link between Catherine Grainger and Kit, the red of her hair liberally sprinkled with silver, her face nowhere near as haughty as Catherine's, but not as youthfully softened as Kit's.

Marcus turned back to Kit.

She gave him a shaky smile, knowing she would no

longer have to explain to him what her connection was to Catherine Grainger, that it was perfectly obvious to anyone seeing the three women together exactly what their relationship was.

But the important thing was that Catherine was here!

After all her coldness on Tuesday morning, her claims of having no interest in the daughter she had disowned twenty-eight years ago, she was here!

As Kit's father had already stated: it was a start...

CHAPTER SIXTEEN

'I SHOULD have known!' Marcus whispered at Kit's side. The two of them were sitting in the relatives' room, after Kit had gone in briefly to speak to her mother before leaving her alone with Tom and Catherine. The look on Heather's face had been both hopeful and apprehensive when she had seen just who was accompanying her husband.

'Why should you?' Kit responded. 'As far as you were aware, there was absolutely no connection between myself and Catherine Grainger.'

'Except the fact that she's your grandmother!' Marcus returned, obviously still completely poleaxed by that fact.

'Not really.' Kit wrinkled her nose at the thought. 'Never having had a grandmother, I've always thought of them as little old ladies who live in cottages and knit tea cosies and things like that; hardly an accurate description of Catherine!'

'Hardly,' Marcus allowed.

Kit could see by the expression on his face that he was still having difficulty coming to terms with the fact that Catherine was her grandmother. 'Catherine is my mother's mother, yes. But she's denied the fact for the last twenty-eight years.'

'Something you decided to change on Tuesday,' Marcus observed. 'That's why you were at Grainger International that afternoon, isn't it?'

Kit gave a shiver as she remembered that conversation with Catherine. 'She was so horrible. I had no idea a mother could be so hard and unyielding towards her only child!'

'But she's here now, Kit,' Marcus reminded her.

'Yes—and if she says or does anything to upset my mother, then my father is never going to forgive me for bringing her back into our lives!' Kit said with certainty.

Kit was well aware that her father adored her—both her parents had always been wonderful with her. But nevertheless she had always known that her mother and father shared a very special love, the sort of love that needed no one else.

Perhaps that was what Catherine had sensed all those years ago, sensed and resented?

'I don't think Catherine has come here to cause trouble,' Marcus reassured her.

But while he had continued to be supportive since Catherine's arrival at the clinic, Kit sensed a certain remoteness in him now that hadn't been there before, a distancing, as if he wished himself far away from here. And her.

'I hope not.' Kit still felt uncertain about that. 'But— Marcus, I'd never even met her until last weekend at Desmond Hayes's house,' she explained.

'Amazing!'

'Yes,' Kit agreed. 'I have always known she was my grandmother, of course, but—I couldn't believe it when I saw her there!'

'It must have taken a lot of courage for you to enter the lion's den on Tuesday.'

Kit glanced across the corridor to her mother's room.

'What do you think they're saying in there?' she said worriedly, able to hear a low murmur of voices, but not what was actually being said.

'Anybody's guess,' Marcus replied. 'But if Catherine's got any sense whatsoever she will take the second chance she's been given and grasp it with both hands!'

Kit gave him a searching look, wondering if there was any hidden meaning to that statement—after all, he was here too, wasn't he…? But Marcus's expression was as unreadable as ever.

She sighed at the barrier she sensed he had deliberately put up. 'That certainly wasn't the impression Catherine gave me when I left her office on Tuesday. She—' She broke off as the door across the corridor opened and Catherine came out and crossed the hallway to join them in the relatives' room.

Catherine's normally composed face seemed ravaged by emotion; for once she looked every one of her sixty-seven years. Just how had the meeting with Heather gone…?

'Can I get you a coffee or tea, Catherine?' Marcus offered as he stood up.

The older woman looked at him as if seeing him for the first time. 'A whisky would probably be more beneficial!' she answered shakily.

'Sorry.' Marcus grimaced apologetically as he indicated the machine in the corner of the room. 'There's only tea or coffee.'

'Coffee, then. Black. No sugar. Thank you,' Catherine added belatedly, suddenly dropping down onto one of the chairs to bury her face in her hands.

Kit hesitated only fractionally before moving to sit

on the chair beside Catherine and put her arm around her grandmother's shaking shoulders, deciding she didn't care whether or not Catherine welcomed her attention; she was going to get it, anyway!

Marcus placed the coffee on the table beside Catherine before turning to Kit. 'I think it might be better if I go now and leave the two of you alone to talk—'

'No!' Kit instantly looked up to protest. 'You said you would stay, Marcus,' she reminded him, sure now that she hadn't imagined that distance he was once again putting between them.

'I did, yes, but—' He broke off, drawing in a deeply ragged breath. 'I'm sure you and Catherine must have a lot of things you need to talk about. In private.'

Kit felt sure that if he left now, despite what he had said earlier, she was never going to see him again.

'Stay, Marcus,' Catherine was the one to plead with him now as she raised her head to look at him. 'Some of what I have to say concerns you as well as Kit.'

His eyes widened. 'It does?'

'Yes,' Catherine confirmed. 'Strange as it may seem...yes.'

'Please do stay, Marcus.' Kit added her own plea to Catherine's; she couldn't imagine what the older woman might have to say that involved Marcus, but she wanted him to stay, anyway; *they* still had a lot to say to one other!

'Okay.' He dropped down into a chair on the other side of the room from the two women, his expression guarded as he looked across at them.

Kit could have cried for the ever widening gap that

seemed to be growing between them, but could think of nothing to say that might close it.

'Very well.' Catherine straightened in her chair, composing her features into their usual calmness. 'You may have wondered, Marcus, why over the years I have attempted to subvert certain business deals that your father, and subsequently yourself, have been interested in...?'

'You mean this has been going on for longer than the last six months?' Kit gasped, at the same time giving Marcus a frowning look.

'Well...to give Marcus his due, he may not have been aware of it until the last six months or so,' Catherine allowed. 'His father and his uncle Simon ran the company until his uncle's death ten years ago.'

Then she spoke to Marcus once again. 'After that, it was your father and yourself, and since your father's retirement just over a year ago you have managed the company alone.'

'Yes...' Marcus confirmed warily.

'Forty years ago I was in love with your uncle Simon,' Catherine told him flatly.

Marcus looked stunned. 'But—but forty years ago he would have been married to my aunt Stella, with a young daughter.'

'Yes,' Catherine acknowledged emotionlessly. 'And I was a young widow, with my own daughter, and my dead husband's ailing business to run. But Simon and I fell in love, anyway.'

Marcus was listening intently. 'What happened?'

Catherine smiled humourlessly. 'What usually happens; Simon decided to stay with his wife and child!'

'And you have carried on some sort of vendetta

against Marcus's family ever since…?' Kit guessed, incredulous.

'It wasn't quite like that,' Catherine told her. 'But— yes, I suppose that's more or less what I have done. I really loved Simon, you see, but it wasn't enough to hold him. Maitland Enterprises was already a very successful business, and Simon was sure that if he left his wife and child to be with me that James—your father…' she gave an inclination of her head in Marcus's direction '…would cut him out of the business, as well as the family.'

'Forty years ago he probably would have done,' Marcus conceded softly.

'Yes,' Catherine sighed. 'So after Simon left me, I put all my time and energy into bringing up my daughter and making a success of my business. It thrived— and at the age of nineteen my daughter decided she was madly in love with a man old enough to be her father!'

'More to the point,' Marcus was the one to put in quietly, 'a man who loved her as deeply?'

'Yes,' Catherine acknowledged shakily. 'Tom McGuire was a penniless, middle-aged artist—and anyone with eyes in their head could see that my daughter loved him, and he loved her, with a love that transcended any obstacle that might stop them being together!'

'They still love each other in that way,' Kit told her huskily, the tears once again swimming in her eyes.

'I know.' Catherine reached out tentatively and touched Kit's hand briefly. 'And I, my dear—as you pointed out so clearly on Tuesday—am a silly old woman,' she said tremulously.

'Oh, but—'

'No one has ever spoken to me in the way that you did on Tuesday.' Catherine gave a rueful smile. 'Maybe if they had I wouldn't have been so stupid as to allow that one unhappy love affair to sour the rest of my life, to deprive me, not only of my daughter for twenty-eight years, but also my—my granddaughter.' She drew in a shaky breath. 'Kit, I told you on Tuesday that I had no need of a granddaughter, but I was wrong. So very wrong!'

Kit looked into eyes so like her mother's now they were softened with emotion, so like her own, that it was impossible to withstand the pleading for forgiveness she could see there.

She moved tentatively towards this woman, her grandmother. Catherine seemed to move at exactly the same time, and the two of them were soon in each other's arms.

'She will be all right, won't she, Kit?' Catherine murmured brokenly some time later. 'All these years I've missed, all this time, and now—'

'She will be all right,' Kit said with much more certainty than she actually felt, knowing Catherine needed to hear that at this moment.

'Ladies,' Marcus intervened. 'I think it's time for you to go back in to see Heather.' He indicated Tom standing in the doorway waiting for them all to accompany him back into Heather's room.

It wasn't all settled between her mother and her grandmother—Kit wasn't naïve enough to be believe that it was—but she felt certain that the two of them had made a lot of headway towards an understanding today.

If only she and Marcus could do the same…!

'If you'll all excuse me…?' Marcus stood up, his expression once more remote.

Kit stood up. 'Do you have to go?'

His eyes were darkly unfathomable as he met her gaze. 'Yes, I really do have to go,' he confirmed, turning away before hesitating and turning back again. 'You'll let me know? How things go?' he asked.

'Yes, of course,' she confirmed breathlessly, wishing she could persuade him to stay, wishing he would stay; if she needed anyone today it was the man she loved. 'I'll call you later, shall I?' she said stiffly.

'Do that,' Marcus accepted. 'Catherine. Tom.' Then he left without a backward glance.

Kit's eyes instantly burned with the tears that were so near the surface of her emotions today. Marcus had said he would stay, that he would be here for her, but all that had seemed to change once he had realised Catherine was her grandmother.

But why? Why was he here at all today? He hadn't explained anything!

But it was time to go in and talk to her mother now, to offer the love and support she knew she needed. There would be time later for her to think of the pain of Marcus's abrupt departure.

'Go after him, Kit.'

She turned to look at the woman who was her grandmother, the two of them back in the waiting room. Her father was by the bedside of his beloved wife, last seen kissing her hands with all of the pent-up emotion of the last five hours as Heather came round from her operation.

It had been a success! A complete and utter success. Heather was still incredibly sleepy, but out of danger, so the surgeon had told them all a short time ago.

In fact everything looked so much more positive to Kit than it had this morning, her mother and grandmother reconciled, the operation over and successful. The only thing keeping her from jumping with joy was the fact that Marcus had left them without a backward glance.

'Sorry?' She turned to Catherine blankly.

The older woman smiled encouragingly. 'I said go after him, Kit. Don't make the same mistakes I did. Maybe if I had put up more of a fight for Simon...'

'It isn't the same.' Kit smiled as she tried to hide the misery that was consuming her.

She shouldn't feel like this; her mother had survived the operation, was going to be completely well again, and that was all that really mattered, not her foolish love for Marcus.

Catherine gave a rueful smile back. 'You're right, it isn't—I believe Marcus really is in love with you!'

'No—'

'Oh, yes,' Catherine persisted. 'I knew it when I saw him here with you this morning.'

Kit shook her head. 'He just felt sorry for me—'

'Now you're being silly, Kit,' Catherine rebuked with some of her old sharpness. 'You're beautiful. Accomplished—'

'Your granddaughter,' Kit put in.

Catherine's eyes widened. 'And what does that have to do with anything?'

'Everything, I would have thought!'

'Don't be ridiculous,' Catherine bridled. 'Okay, so I accept that was probably a bit of a shock for him—'

'"A bit of a shock"!' Kit echoed. 'You have no idea!'

'Oh, but I think that I have—'

'Kit.'

She turned sharply at the sound of Marcus's voice, completely surprised to find him standing in the open doorway.

'I think I can take it from here, Catherine,' he told the older woman, although his expression was once again guarded as he turned back to Kit. 'I had the surgeon's secretary inform me as soon as the operation was over. I'm so glad everything turned out well.'

Kit swallowed hard, her head still spinning from the fact that he had come back. 'Thank you,' was all she could manage.

'If you'll excuse us for a few minutes, Catherine?' Marcus spoke briskly. 'I have a few things I need to say to Kit.'

'More than a few, I should have thought,' Catherine commented derisively.

'Perhaps,' he allowed coolly. 'Kit?' his voice softened noticeably.

It was that very gentleness in his tone that persuaded her into going with him. 'You'll explain to my father when he comes back?' she prompted Catherine. 'I shouldn't be long.'

'Of course,' Catherine agreed. 'Oh, and by the way, Marcus...' She stopped them as Kit would have followed Marcus from the room. 'I had a visit from your lawyer this morning—'

'Ex-lawyer,' Marcus put in harshly.

Catherine gave a gracious inclination of her head. 'He seemed to be of the opinion that I might offer him a job.'

'An opinion you quickly disillusioned him of, I'm sure,' Marcus rejoined.

'Of course,' Catherine confirmed graciously. 'I only ever employ people whose loyalty I can be completely sure of.'

'So do I,' Marcus returned sardonically.

Lewis. They had to be talking about Lewis. And if Lewis had gone to Catherine for a job after Marcus had sacked him—!

It suddenly all became clear. In fact, Kit could kick herself for not having realised before. And maybe if she hadn't been so agitated this morning then she might have done! Lewis had to have been the one passing confidential information on to Catherine all the time!

And Marcus had to have known that this morning in order to dismiss Lewis...

Marcus hadn't been with her today because he cared about her, he had just felt guilty for having wrongly accused her.

'I think this is far enough, don't you?' she said woodenly once they stood outside in the car park. 'Just make your apology and then I can go back inside. I take it you are going to apologize again for the mistake you obviously made?'

Marcus closed his eyes briefly. 'It isn't the way you think, Kit—'

'Isn't it?' Her eyes flashed deeply grey. 'I thought you cared, really cared, and instead you're just feeling

foolish for having made a mistake. Well, you can take
your apology and—'

'Kit…!' he groaned throatily.

'I'm sorry if that isn't ladylike enough for you—but
it's the best you're going to get!' She was shaking with
anger now, feeling utterly foolish herself for ever har-
bouring any hopes where this man was concerned.
'Yes, it's true that Catherine Grainger is my grandmother. It's also true that until last weekend I had never
met her. But even if that weren't the case, I worked
for you.' She glared at him. 'I would never have betrayed your confidence in me. Never!' She inwardly
cursed herself as her voice broke emotionally.

Marcus's hands were clenched at his sides. 'It's also
true that when I came to your apartment Tuesday evening I still didn't know Lewis was the one responsible
for those security leaks; I didn't find that out until I
confronted him with it first thing this morning,' he told
her directly. 'It's what I thought on Tuesday when I
arranged that meeting with Catherine, had hoped to see
the two of them together and then confront them with
it. Instead I found myself face to face with you…!'

Kit already knew how damning that had looked;
hadn't her heart been breaking ever since?

'I didn't know what to think any more,' Marcus continued. 'I wanted to believe you, but the evidence
against you was so damning. But I came back on
Tuesday night anyway, Kit. I couldn't have stayed
away, not once Penny had told me you were upset—
and not just because of me,' he added firmly as Kit
would have spoken. 'Kit, I came back,' he repeated
determinedly.

She looked at him searchingly now, that barrier no

longer there, all his emotions, everything he was feeling reflected there in his eyes. 'Why?' she finally breathed, hardly daring to move as she waited for his answer.

'You know why, Kit,' he said.

She knew the reason why she wanted him to have come back; she just wasn't sure it was his…

'I love you!' he groaned as he saw the continuing doubts in her eyes. 'I've loved you since I first saw Kit McGuire as she really is and not as she wanted me to see her. Before that I knew you to be a capable and efficient PA, but without the disguise—'

'I told you, it wasn't a disguise!' she defended, but not with the same heat as before, her own barriers starting to crumble.

'Without the defences, then,' he amended. 'You were beautiful, and desirable, and completely adorable. I love you, Kit. I left the clinic earlier because I thought—I realised, once I had seen your mother and Catherine, that I should get out of your life, get out and stay out, that I don't deserve to have you forgive me. My only excuse is that it's because I love you that I reacted as strongly as I did. I know that's no excuse, not really, but— No matter what happens between us in the future, you deserve to know that I love you more than life itself.'

'"No matter what happens between us"…?' she repeated.

'If you tell me to go away, to stay away—' He broke off. 'If you turn me away, Kit, I will still love you. And go on loving you. Always.'

In the same way that her parents had always loved each other…!

She looked at him, deliberately holding his gaze as her tongue moistened her lips. 'And if I don't tell you to go away?'

His gaze was fixed on the moistness of her mouth now. 'Then I'll ask you to marry me. And pray,' he added.

Marcus loved her? Wanted to marry her?

Her eyes began to glow, the ice that had settled about her heart quickly melting. 'Well?' she prompted huskily.

His dark gaze held hers. 'Kit, I know I don't deserve your forgiveness—'

'Skip that bit.' She gave a shaky smile. 'In future I promise not to keep secrets from you, particularly damning ones,' she vowed.

'But I should have believed you—'

'Why should you?' she interrupted. 'Even I know how bad it must have looked.' She tilted her head. 'I'm still waiting, Marcus,' she reminded him, encouraged by the love she could see burning in his eyes.

Marcus took hold of her hand, his fingers tightening about hers before he went down on one knee in front of her. 'Kit, will you marry me?'

'Get up!' she told him hurriedly, aware, even if he didn't appear to be, that it had rained some time during the last few hours, and that the pavement was wet beneath the knee of his expensively tailored trousers.

'Not until you answer me,' he told her stubbornly.

Marry Marcus? Spend the rest of her life with him, loving him, and being loved in return?

'Marry me, Kit.' He looked up at her intensely. 'Marry me and I swear I will never again doubt a single word you ever say to me!'

She could see that he meant it too, for the first time noticing the evidence of his own pain the last two days, lines etched beside his eyes and mouth that hadn't been there before.

'I do love you, Marcus,' she declared.

His eyes flared with emotion, his hand tightening on hers. 'Then say you'll marry me!'

She gave a choked laugh. 'If you get up from the pavement I promise I'll marry you,' she bargained.

'Good enough.' He rose to his feet, his arms moving about the slenderness of her waist, his eyes blazing with love as he looked down at her. 'As soon as your mother is well enough to attend we'll be married, yes?'

'Yes,' she agreed unhesitantly before his mouth claimed hers and she lost herself in the wonder of his kiss, knowing that, like her mother before her, she had found the one man she loved and wanted to spend the rest of her life with.

And who, despite their rather shaky start, loved and wanted to spend the rest of his life with her.

Love.

It really was the only thing that mattered.

A Special Offer from

HARLEQUIN *Presents*

This August, purchase 6 Harlequin Presents books and get these THREE books for FREE!

ONE NIGHT WITH THE TYCOON
by Lee Wilkinson

IN THE MILLIONAIRE'S POSSESSION
by Sara Craven

THE MILLIONAIRE'S MARRIAGE CLAIM
by Lindsay Armstrong

To receive your THREE FREE BOOKS, send us 6 (six) proofs of purchase
from August Harlequin Presents books to the addresses below.

In the U.S.:	In Canada:
Presents Free Book Offer	Presents Free Book Offer
P.O. Box 9057	P.O. Box 622
Buffalo, NY	Fort Erie, ON
14269-9057	L2A 5X3

Name (PLEASE PRINT)

Address   Apt. #

City   State/Prov.   Zip/Postal Code

098 KKJ DXJN

Presents
Free Book
Offer
PROOF OF
PURCHASE
HPPOPAUG06

www.eHarlequin.com

HARLEQUIN *Presents*

Dinner at 8...
Don't be late!

He's suave and sophisticated,
He's undeniably charming.
And above all, he treats her like a lady.

But don't be fooled....

Beneath the tux, there's a primal passionate
lover, who's determined to make her his!

Wined, dined and swept away by a British billionaire!

If you enjoyed what you just read,
then we've got an offer you can't resist!

Take 2 bestselling
love stories FREE!

Plus get a FREE surprise gift!

Clip this page and mail it to Harlequin Reader Service®

IN U.S.A.	**IN CANADA**
3010 Walden Ave.	P.O. Box 609
P.O. Box 1867	Fort Erie, Ontario
Buffalo, N.Y. 14240-1867	L2A 5X3

YES! Please send me 2 free Harlequin Presents® novels and my free surprise gift. After receiving them, if I don't wish to receive anymore, I can return the shipping statement marked cancel. If I don't cancel, I will receive 6 brand-new novels every month, before they're available in stores! In the U.S.A., bill me at the bargain price of $3.80 plus 25¢ shipping & handling per book and applicable sales tax, if any*. In Canada, bill me at the bargain price of $4.47 plus 25¢ shipping & handling per book and applicable taxes**. That's the complete price and a savings of at least 10% off the cover prices—what a great deal! I understand that accepting the 2 free books and gift places me under no obligation ever to buy any books. I can always return a shipment and cancel at any time. Even if I never buy another book from Harlequin, the 2 free books and gift are mine to keep forever.

106 HDN DZ7Y
306 HDN DZ7Z

Name	(PLEASE PRINT)	
Address	Apt.#	
City	State/Prov.	Zip/Postal Code

Not valid to current Harlequin Presents® subscribers.

Want to try two free books from another series?
Call 1-800-873-8635 or visit www.morefreebooks.com.

* Terms and prices subject to change without notice. Sales tax applicable in N.Y.
** Canadian residents will be charged applicable provincial taxes and GST.
All orders subject to approval. Offer limited to one per household.
® are registered trademarks owned and used by the trademark owner and or its licensee.

PRES04R   ©2004 Harlequin Enterprises Limited